MacIntyre's
IMPROBABLE
BESTIARY

Perverse Verse & Odious Odes by
F. GWYNPLAINE MacINTYRE

with *Editorial Input, Output, Throughput*
& Unmitigated Interference from the likes of
Darrell Schweitzer
for which the author will eternally
pretend to be grateful.

WILDSIDE PRESS & ZADOK ALLEN: PUBLISHERS
Pennsylvania

MacIntyre's Improbable Bestiary

A catalog of this and other books may be obtained from the
Wildside Press web site: **www.wildsidepress.com**

First edition: May, 2001

*This Bestiary is dedicated
in affectionate memory,
and with infinite love,
to*
Lenore Marie Nier MacIntyre
*(1944–1993):
my Muse, my Enchantress,
my Brown-Eyed Raccoon.*

Also by **F. Gwynplaine MacIntyre**:

The Woman Between the Worlds
(ISBN 0-595-08884-8)
Available from iUniverse Books at **www.iuniverse.com**

A Pest Iamb, Anapest I'll Be

☞ *Or . . . you too can be a Poet, if you are willing to spend your days*
Drunk & Penniless, babbling incoherently Face-Downwards in yᵉ Gutter,
whence you will be Sentenced to yᵉ Workhouse, where you will
wallow amidst yᵉ Filth, to die Shrieking & Gibbering,
and then spend yᵉ Eternity thereafter tormented
in yᵉ Hellfire & Brimstone for all Time to Come.
Ah, but your poems will be ~~immoral~~ (pardon yᵉ Typo) immortal.

I am a passionate advocate of poetry that *rhymes*. Allow me to paraphrase the great Ira Gershwin, who was a published poet before he began writing song lyrics:

> *I'm writing in rhyme,*
> *'Cos that's the kind of guy I'm.*

This book is not about me, so I shan't bore you with my life story. For poetic purposes, here's all you need to know about me:

◆ As you might guess from the name *MacIntyre*, I am Scottish by birth. One of Scotland's greatest poets was the Argyllshire bard Duncan Ban MacIntyre (1724 – 1812), who wrote *Mic Coiseam* and *Coire Cheathaich* and many other lovely Gaelic ballads. Not all MacIntyres are related, but I hope that I'm a descendant of yon Duncan. I do not claim to be a blue-blooded aristocrat. On the contrary: the colour of my blood is *tartan plaid*.

◆ I am Australian by upbringing. Despite what you saw in **Mad Max** and the **'Crocodile' Dundee** movies, Australia is quite civilised. Education is compulsory by law, and the national literacy rate is just a wallaby's eyelash below 100%. It's not likely that anyone would be Australian *and* illiterate both at the same go . . . and yet somehow I managed to be both.

When I was a wee bairn in the 1950s, schoolrooms in Australia's outback were few and far between. Many outback children took their school lessons via short-wave radio, from a teacher at a central transmitting station in Alice Springs. I spent my formative years in

I

rural regions of central and northern Australia, and I had little access to schoolbooks or radios. So I didn't learn to read until I was within hailing distance of puberty.

Since I didn't know how to read or write, I had only one method of data storage: *memory*. Any information which I hoped to retain had to be memorised, or it was lost forever.

In trying to strengthen my memory, I made the happy discoveries of *rhyme* and *metre*.* Information could be memorised more easily if I arranged my data-stream into metric verses that *rhymed*. I trained myself to organise my thoughts — as completely as possible — into rhymed units of regular metre.

Eventually, of course, I learnt to read and write . . . and to walk erect without dragging my knuckles. And yet my early rhyme-habit stayed with me, so that to this day I often *think in rhyme*. Often, when I am surprised or startled, I instinctively react by thinking and speaking <u>in rhymed verse</u>. Two brief examples:

❏ Southwest of London is a large outdoor labyrinth known as the Hampton Court Maze: it is a popular tourist attraction. Quite nearby is a Tudor palace formerly occupied by Henry VIII. One day in 1986, a friend gave me the shocking news that Hampton Court Palace had just been damaged in a serious fire. I immediately asked: *'Did the blaze reach the Maze?'*

❏ More recently, I dined with friends at a seafood restaurant in Manhattan. One of my table companions made a bizarre statement — I do not know if it was true — to the effect that the seafood in most New York City restaurants is supplied by organised-crime figures. I nodded sagely and muttered: *'Lobster mobsters.'* This same tablemate then alleged that one gang of criminals will sometimes hijack a rival gang's shipments of seafood. I nodded once more and replied: *'Oyster hoisters.'*†

---

* 'Metre' is, of course, the British spelling for the word which an American poet would spell 'meter'. (Assuming that the American poet is able to spell.) In Britain, a metre is never a *meter* unless coins go into it or gas comes out of it. This explains why the Beatles song is not called 'Lovely Rita Metre Maid'.

Speaking of spelling, the British spelling of the word 'anapest' would actually be *anapæst* . . . but I decided to use the American spelling in the title of this foreword. Throughout this book, I will oscillate between British and American spellings, as the fancy takes me. Do I contradict myself? Yes, I don't.

† I do not know if seafood thieves will mussel into one another's territory. But this would certainly be an example of shellfish behaviour.

2

Now we come to the Improbable Bestiary.

Why a Bestiary? In mediæval times, poets assembled sets of cautionary verses. Each verse described a different beast, and offered comments (approvingly or otherwise) on the creature's behaviour or its appearance. There was always a Very Important Moral lurking in the underbrush. For example, a poem about the Bee would encourage Industriousness. A poem about the Pig would condemn Gluttony. Any self-respecting Bestiary was expected to serve a High Moral Purpose.

None of that High Moral Purpose crap will be found *here*, folks.

In the 1960s, whilst living in London, I fell into the employ of a cabaret double-act known as Flanders and Swann. Donald Swann was an immensely talented musician who later collaborated with J.R.R. Tolkien, setting to music the lyrics and poems from Tolkien's **Lord of the Rings**. Michael Flanders was a nimble mind trapped in earthbound flesh: stricken by polio during his national service in the Coastal Forces, he spent most of his adulthood in a wheelchair.‡ My job consisted largely of helping Flanders commute between his home in Bedford Park and his theatrical engagements. I also had a far less glamorous task to perform, which I shan't describe here except to mention the fact that Flanders was incontinent.§

Among the high spots of Flanders and Swann's cabaret turn were their comic songs about various animals, including the Gnu, the Ostrich, the Chameleon, the Sloth, the Armadillo, and — most notably — the Hippopotamus. These ditties were collected into a songbook titled **The Bestiary of Flanders and Swann**.

---

‡ When not performing his cabaret act with Swann, Flanders occasionally starred in stage productions of *The Man Who Came to Dinner*. The lead rôle in this comedy is Sheridan Whiteside, a bombastic bearded know-all who plays most of his scenes in a wheelchair. Michael Flanders was himself a bombastic bearded know-all, so the rôle came naturally. In deference to Flanders's handicap, the script was slightly rewritten so that *all* of Sheridan Whiteside's scenes were played from a wheelchair.

§ Although Flanders and Swann had a long stage career, they rejected nearly every offer to appear on television. No explanation was ever offered for this reticence. So I now reveal the reason for their camera-shyness: the incontinent Flanders was prone to 'accidents'. In cabaret and theatre, the audiences were too far away to notice these mishaps . . . but Flanders was pathologically afraid that the all-seeing eye of a TV camera's zoom lens might capture his facial expression (or some other telling detail) during one of his lapses.

Inspired by Flanders and Swann, I too aspired to become a creative *artiste* (this word is pronounced 'worthless layabout'). I saw straight away that their Bestiary had an obvious advantage. Whenever Flanders and Swann needed fresh subject matter for another song, they had only to ask themselves: 'Right, what animal haven't we done yet?' And . . . *voilà!* they had the topic for their next opus. Unless they exhausted the entire list of animal species — from the Aardvark to the Zykzyk¶ — they would always have new subject matter.

I recognised this as a Brilliant Concept, and so of course I stole it. Casting envious eyes upon Flanders and Swann, I vowed that I too would one day create a Bestiary.

In the meantime, I became aware of other Bestiaries. I savoured **The Bad Child's Book of Beasts** and **More Beasts for Worse Children**, the comic verse collections by Hilaire Belloc. I also discovered **Prefabulous Animiles** by the English poet James Reeves: a book that some clever publisher will one day profitably rescue from undeserved obscurity. Reeves's mythical monsters are wholly original, and truly delightful. **The Bab Ballads**, written and illustrated by W.S. Gilbert,** are masterpieces of comedy: these too inspired my own efforts.

The influences that shaped me were not exclusively British. I was profoundly influenced by the American poets Sara Teasdale and Guy Wetmore Carryl, and also by the Bengali-born artist/poet Sukumar Ray, whose uniquely demented nonsense verses were perfectly matched by his whimsical illustrations.

I also encountered, of course, Lewis Carroll.

The author of **Alice in Wonderland** had two favourite pastimes. One of these, alas, involved taking photographs of little girls naked. (The *girls* were naked; Lewis Carroll kept his clothes on.) Carroll's other pastime was his penchant for taking long walks, in all sorts of weather. During one of his walks, Lewis Carroll fancied that he heard a voice which spoke a single cryptic line:

'For the Snark was a Boojum, you see.'

¶ I haven't the faintest idea. Go away.

** By an interesting coincidence, *two* of the greatest works in science-fiction literature were inspired by W.S. Gilbert's comic drawings. An illustration in *The Bab Ballads* inspired H.G. Wells to write **The Invisible Man**, and one of Gilbert's illustrations for *Iolanthe* gave Isaac Asimov the inspiration for his **Foundation** series.

Carroll had no idea what this meant. But he knew what to do with it. By the time he reached home, he had composed in his mind an entire verse concluding with this line. This verse in turn became the ending of a long mock-epic poem, which Carroll published as **The Hunting of the Snark**. If you haven't read it, do so immediately. Even better: make every effort to locate Boris Karloff's recording of *The Hunting of the Snark*,†† so that you can have the pleasure of hearing Karloff read it to you. (Again, some clever publisher ought to reissue this . . . and reap the profits accordingly.)

In 1979, while attending that year's edition of the World Science Fiction Convention in Brighton, England, I spent a fateful afternoon conversing with Arthur C. Clarke in the saloon bar of the Brighton Metropole. Sir Arthur (as he later became) had long been interested in *cryptozoology*: the study of beasts that *might* exist, but which haven't yet been hunted down and put into cages. Our conversation was chockablock with crypto-critters such as the Loch Ness Monster, the Abominable Snowman, the Ogopogo, the Bunyip and the Yowie. My mind was full of this monstrous menagerie, then, as I returned to my lodgings at the Old Ship Hotel. (This excellent hotel, by the way, is also the establishment where Sting worked as a bellboy in the film *Quadrophenia*.) As I approached the Old Ship's front door, I seemed to hear a disembodied voice which spoke a single phrase:

'Behold the bashful Yeti.'

Where this voice came from, I know not. Possibly it was the same voice which had accosted Lewis Carroll. At all events, I knew a good line when I heard one. Before I reached my hotel room, the poem of the Yeti was complete in my mind. You'll find that poem in these pages. Within the hour, I was inspired to write several more verses for other mythical beasts: the Centaur, the Unicorn, the Martian.

When the dust settled, I recalled how I had coveted the creations of Flanders and Swann . . . and I realised that *I had begun a Bestiary* uniquely my own. Flanders and Swann gave me the early inspiration. Belloc and Reeves and others nurtured my ambition. Arthur C. Clarke, all unknowing, lit the blue touchpaper and ignited the fuse.

You now hold the result in your hands, feet, or pseudopods.

I am indebted to many authors. My poem *'The Thing in the Jar'* was inspired by Ray Bradbury's classic story *'The Jar'*. Elsewhere in

---

†† The phonograph recording is Cædmon TC 1075, and the audiocassette version is Cædmon CDL 51075. Good hunting.

these pages, 'The Martian' was inspired by several tales in Bradbury's **Martian Chronicles**. My poem 'The Vanishing Man' was inspired by 'Jim Jay', a science-fiction poem by Walter de la Mare, an Englishman whose poetry deserves widespread attention.

Most of the poems in **MacIntyre's Improbable Bestiary** were first published in *Isaac Asimov's Science Fiction Magazine*, *Weird Tales*, *Amazing Stories* or other charivaria. If you will take the trouble (please <u>don't!</u>) to locate those old magazines in some back-number bookstall, and compare the yellowing originals of my poems with their present incarnations in this volume, you will see that I have tweaked the odd line here and there. My poetry is not graven in stone, and I have indulged my urge to make a few revisions.

Ideally, poetry should be read aloud, in the bardic tradition . . . but this begs the question of pronunciation. Having spent much of my adult life in Wales (where they take their bards *very* seriously indeed) and in England, my inner muse speaks with a British accent. But most of these poems were written for American publications — and with American readers in mind — so Yank pronunciations will occur throughout these pages. For instance, in 'The Gremlin and the Glitch':

> *. . . she shoots croquet*
> *With the Milky Way.*

or, in 'The Ogre':

> *And they pulled Johnny free*
> *From beneath the debris.*

Here, the rhymes demand American pronunciations of *croquet* and *debris*: respectively, 'cro-KAY' and 'de-BREE'. In Britain and Australia, these words are typically pronounced 'CRO-kay' and 'DEB-ree' . . . so the rhyme will be lost for British readers.

Conversely, my science-fiction song lyric 'Donovan's Mikado' (also reprinted in this volume) requires a *British* pronunciation of the word 'data', because I was parodying an English original. I try to cater for readers on <u>both</u> sides of the Atlantic.

I am proud of the fact that — with very few exceptions — each of the poems and lyrics in this collection *tells a story*, with a beginning and a middle and an end. This is vastly superior to the techniques employed by purveyors of twinkle-dinkle verse forms such as *Haiku*. The whole point of *haiku* is to write a poem in which absolutely nothing happens. Here is a typical haiku:

Big brown cow-patty
Stinking up the whole meadow.
Deeply meaningful.

Various modern and postmodern *artistes* (this word is pronounced 'pretentious git-wits') have greeted my poems with hoots of derision, because I insist on adhering to the 'outmoded' and 'archaic' rules of *rhyme* and *metre*. The minions of Political Correctness repeatedly inform me that rhyme and metre are relics of the dim past, and should be left there. I disagree.

If poetry is to have any future at all, that future depends on Rhyme and Metre.

Some fortunate few people have a talent which enables them to perform before an audience. These talented people become Actresses or Jugglers or Ventriloquists or Rope Dancers. But there are other people who possess no discernible talent, yet who insist upon having an audience anyway. These untalented people call themselves Performance Artists. They smear their naked bodies with chocolate, and thrust rutabagas into their fundaments whilst shrieking gibberish about Ronald Reagan or Margaret Thatcher. These 'artists' are financed by arts-council grants, which came out of the wallets of honest taxpayers . . . including *you*, Gentle Reader.

In much the same way, there are people who have no discernible talent for *writing*, yet who insist on writing anyway. They cannot craft Literature or Drama or any sort of prose narrative. So they write incoherent claptrap that doesn't rhyme, serves no metric form, tells no story . . . and they call it Poetry. Or <u>Modern</u> Poetry. Or, worst of all, <u>Post</u>modern Poetry . . . whatever that may be. Like the swindlers in the story of the Emperor's New Clothes, these self-appointed poets hold up their worthless handiwork and assure us that — if we fail to see its merits — the fault lies in our perception, not in their artifice.

To this I say: *bull cookies!*

Ask any ten publishers to name the *least* commercial form of writing — the writing that near-as-nowt-to-<u>nobody</u> will pay money to read — and all those publishers will give you the same answer: *Poetry*. So long as pretentious drivel-smiths are permitted to attach the sacred label POETRY to their rhymeless and stumbling vanities, the good people of the book-buying public will (very sensibly) direct their attention — and their money — elsewhere.

In order to save Poetry, we must set high standards for those who would call themselves Poets.

The limerick about the girl from Nantucket will still be in print — and will still be recited, remembered, and cherished — long after the postmodernist lit-critters and their entire unrhyming output have vanished forever, unread and unmourned.

Rhyme-lovers, unite! Let us root out, hoot out, and boot out from Poetry's domain, now and forever, all the bigots who sneer at traditional rhyming poetry and who deride it as 'greeting-card verse'.

Let us mangle, dangle, and strangle those alleged Poets who boast that they 'reject the outmoded concept' of rhyme.

Rhyme and Metre are not shackles to fetter the artistic soul. They are the *framework* — the mast, the armature, the easel — upon which great verse is crafted. Rhyme and Metre are the guideposts on the poet's journey. They are the compass and the chart in every poet's soul and heart.

Without Rhyme, there is no Reason.

F. Gwynplaine MacIntyre
Penrhyndeudraeth,
North Wales, 2001

8

THE YETI

Behold the bashful Yeti, the Himalayan Yeti:
Abominable Snowman in his mountaintop retreat.
The Yeti feels no passion for current vogue or fashion:
He sports no Gucci loafers on his size-eleven feet.

The Yeti always mutinies when faced with public scrutinies;
You'll seldom see him sitting in the pub and sipping ale.
Reporters from the *London News*
And television camera crews
(Who hope he'll grant them interviews)
Inevitably fail.

Behold the bashful Yeti, the misanthropic Yeti:
Elusive and reclusive and a trifle shy is he.
Don't send him invitations to social recreations;
He seldom comes to banquets, and he *never* comes to tea!

The Yeti is so timid, he
Won't come into proximity
Of science expeditions when they shout at him and wave.
The Yeti has no wish to stay
And chat with people such as they;
He'd really rather run away
And hide inside a cave.

So if you see a Yeti — a shy, retiring Yeti —
Just smile and keep on walking; that's the proper thing to do.
Don't call him names or tease him,
Or do things that displease him;
You really wouldn't like it if a Yeti bothered *you!*

Originally published in *Isaac Asimov's Science Fiction Magazine*, June 1981.

The Martian

Well, our rocket ship from Earth had accidentally run aground;
We were stranded on the barren Martian plain.
So while Joe sent a distress call, I said I would look around:
Reconnoitering the craters and terrain.
I saw rocks and dying land, tons of reddish Martian sand,
So much emptiness: it almst seemed a pity.
Then I *saw* it! It was *real*: twisted strands of rusting *steel*,
And a rubble heap that must have been a CITY!
Then I heard someone speak, in a voice that was weak
And a tone full of worry and fright . . .
And I turned to see who — was it one of the crew? —
But there wasn't a person in sight . . .
There was nobody there, yet the pink Martian air
Seemed to echo a faraway call:
"I'm the very last Martian,
the very last Martian,
the very last Martian of all . . ."

Then I heard something move in the shadows behind me,
And thought that the crew had sent someone to find me.
I turned, and I saw something there.
But it wasn't a crewman: *the thing wasn't human!*
It crawled through the dust in despair . . .
I heard words in my brain, full of sorrow and pain,
As the thing crept along in its crawl:
"I'm the very last Martian,
the very last Martian,
the very last Martian of all . . ."

Originally published in *Isaac Asimov's Science Fiction Magazine*, November 1981.

"Long ago," the thing said, shaping words in my head,
"We were healthy and strong, and our planet was red
And our cities rose up to the sky.
Then the ground turned to dust, and our cities to rust,
And I watched all my family die . . .
You're from Earth, are you, man? Tell me this if you can:
All my people are dead! Tell me . . . WHY?"
And I wished I knew what to reply . . .

Then the Martian crawled away. There was nothing I could say,
And I went and joined my shipmates not much later.
"We've been found!" said Joe. "Hooray!
Rescue ships are on the way!"
Then he asked me what I'd seen beyond the crater.
"Only dust," I replied. "Dust and shadows," I lied.
"Well, come on: let's get out of this place."
Then I whispered a prayer to the thin Martian air
For the Martian and all of its race.

Well, the days became a year, and I've got a fine career
Flying colonists from Marsport to the station.
Now I supervise a crew; there's a lot of work to do,
Terraforming Mars for human habitation.
But sometimes, late at night, when the twin moons shine bright,
And the Fleet ships roar off into space
I imagine I hear ancient words full of fear,
Ancient sounds from a faraway place.
I can hear the refrain on the high Martian plain,
In a voice that is distant and small:
"I'm the very last Martian,
        the very last Martian . . ."
                And then I hear silence.
                That's all.

I was inspired to write *'The Martian'* after reading Ray Bradbury's
The Martian Chronicles. Thank you, Mister Bradbury.

The very first Bestiary poem which I wrote was 'The Yeti', but
— by chance — the first one to be *published* was 'The Centaur'.
It was also nominated (*ahem!*) for the 1980 Rhysling Award for
best science-fiction or fantasy poem of the year.

THE CENTAUR

The creature called the Centaur (as you may already know)
From head to hips is human, but equestrian below.
And thus he has a problem you might notice at a glance:
He cannot wear a suit unless it has two pairs of pants.
His top half dines on mutton chops, the bottom favors hay.
And so, perforce, their dinner course brings mutual dismay
Because, you see, they can't agree on what to eat which way.
(When offered pie, one end votes *"Aye!"*
The other end says *"Neigh!"*)

If front and back both want a snack, they find themselves unable:
When one end picks up knife and fork and seats itself at table,
The end that votes for hay and oats is halfway to the stable.
(This doesn't make much sense, but bear in mind it's just a fable.)

The centaur Sagittarius had hobbies vast and various,
And yet he was a flop at every sport he chose to play.
At tennis, golf, and soccer he
Was nothing but a mockery,
And things got even worse when he began to try croquet.
(His feet got in the way.)

"I may not be the type," he said, "for physical athletics,
Because I'm neither horse nor man . . . so blame it on genetics.
But there *must* be a sport where I've an asset, not a weakness.
Eureka! I'm a thoroughbred! I'll sign up for the Preakness!"
And thus came the event that makes
Our Centaur feel so cocky:
His back end won the Derby Stakes,
His front end was the jockey.

Originally published in *Isaac Asimov's Science Fiction Magazine*, November 1980.

The FAUN

Meeting the dawn
With a light burst of lyrical
Greeting, the Faun
Plays his reed-pipes and then
Ponders the worth
Of his midsummer miracle,
Wanders the Earth
Seeking maidens and men.

The miller, the tanner, the goose-girl, the cook . . .
Hear music, far music, seductive and sly.
The ploughman hears laughter and hurries to look:
The Goat-Footed Piper comes wandering by.
The nurse drops her basin, the cleric his book,
The milkmaid her churn, and the shepherd his crook.
And each is enchanted, and all of them drawn
To the magical pipes of the musical Faun.
And they follow the music, the beckoning music.
They follow the Faun and his music and then
They dance to the piper, the Goat-Footed Piper.
They dance, as the piper comes up through the glen.

Lightly, the breeze
Joins the melody, beckoning
Slightly . . . the trees
Seem to whisper the tune;
Spanning the days
To a time beyond reckoning,
Fanning the blaze
Of a midsummer noon . . .

And somewhere, oh somewhere, far-distant, away,
The Faun plays his reed-pipes and winks to the sky
And Time waits suspended in midsummer day
Where love never withers and dreams never die.
Some dawn, in my garden, the reed-pipes will play;
The laugh of the piper will lead me astray
To join all the others who dance on my lawn . . .
And I'll follow, with them, to the Land of the Faun.
And I'll follow the music, the faraway music.
We'll follow the Faun and his music and then
I'll dance to the piper, the Goat-Footed Piper.
We'll dance, as the piper comes up through the glen.

Originally published in *Amazing Stories*, March 1985.

13

The TROLL

In a puddlesome bog, in a muddleglum hole
Full of brackenous blog lived a wartyish Troll,
Who spent his days grumpishly hiding.
He hid in his cellar and tried to ignore
The ghastly intruders who knocked on his door:
The horrible humans who came by the score
To sell him aluminum siding.

"Act now!" said the salesmen, *"and buy, at low cost . . ."*
"I GAVE AT THE OFFICE!" the Troll said. "GET LOST!"
"But this is a product you're certain to try . . ."
"THERE'S NOBODY HOME!" the Troll answered. "GOOD-BYE!"
Twelve salesmen, three postmen, and one Candy-Gram
Were met at the door by a very loud **"SCRAM!"**

One day, overladen with bundles, a maiden
Came into the bog, travel-weary and sore.
With trunks and valises and twenty-six pieces
Of baggage, she knocked on the Troll's oaken door.
"GO HOME!" the Troll screamed at her. "BEAT IT! QUIT STALLING!"
But she stood her ground and replied: "Avon calling . . ."

"I've toiletry notions and after-shave lotions
A Troll of distinction (like *you*, sir) should own.
I've napkins and diapers and fingernail-wipers
And forty-three cases of Eau de Cologne.
I've moustache-remover, a portable Hoover,
A razor that comes with a sharpening-stone . . ."
"HOLD ON!" the Troll bleated. "YOU WIN! I'M DEFEATED!
I'LL BUY THE WHOLE MESS **IF YOU'LL LEAVE ME ALONE!**"

In a pool of perfume, in a sweet-scented hole
Full of creams and colognes lives a wartyish Troll
Whose moans echo off through the distance.
He lurks amid gallons of lilac shampoo,
Six cases of soap, and a hair-dryer too
And hopes that — next time Avon Ladies come through —
He'll show a bit more sales resistance.

Originally published in *Amazing Stories*, March 1983.

14

(This poem was inspired by Ray Bradbury's story 'The Jar')

The Thing in the Jar

Originally published in *Isaac Asimov's Science Fiction Magazine*, December 1981.

The carnival is coming, with horses and a clown.
The jungle cats and acrobats and circus are in town.
The Ferris wheel of shining steel, the shoot-the-rapids ride . . .
And one peculiar-looking tent that's standing to the side:
It's got the *Freak show! Geek show! Utterly unique show!*
No-admittance-given-to-the-squeamish-or-the-weak show!
The two-headed chicken, the eight-legged calf,
And Robert-Roberta, the Great Half-and-Half.
The midget who puffs on a three-foot cigar,
And Wonder of Wonders: *The Thing in the Jar* . . .

It's got eyes and it breathes and it bubbles and seethes
And it floats in a bottle of brine.
Does it think? Does it dream? Can it speak? *Can it scream?*
Is it part of some cosmic design?
All the people who visit and wonder "What *is* it?
A freak? Or a fake? Or a con?"
They may wonder and stare, or give up in despair,
But *the Thing in the Jar floats on, floats on* . . .

"It's an optical illusion . . ." ". . . a genuine Venusian . . ."
    "I swear it's got a *human* face; just look into its eyes . . ."
"I bet it's made of leather . . ." "What holds the thing together?"
    "It *can't* be real, but if it is I hope to God it dies . . ."
Each person who pays to enter and gaze
Will think of the Thing till the end of their days.
It floats through the streams of your nightmares and dreams;
It seeps, and it sleeps, and *it's not what it seems* . . .

The carnival is leaving; the circus doesn't stay.
The carny louts and roustabouts have packed the dreams away.
The wagons load and hit the road, the way they've done for years . . .
And one peculiar caravan is full of dreams and fears:
It's got the *Tent show! Bent show! Ten and twenty-cent show!*
Come-and-see-the-strangest-freaks-that-nature-can-invent show!
The customers paid, and they saw the parade,
And the elephants danced, and the music was played,
But while people grow older and memories fade —
When the carnival's packed up and gone —
In their dreams, one and all, they will always recall
That *the Thing in the Jar floats on, floats on* . . .

THE CHINESE DRAGONS

We
   three
     be
        three
Dragons of Kiangsu:
    Lung Wang Hao,
       Shen-lung Po,
          T'ien Lung Fu.
Those who give us rice cakes, honey cakes and tea,
They shall know good fortune: 'tis our prophecy.

Song of T'ien Lung Fu, green three-clawed dragon, who guards the household:

Sentry of the house and keeper of the portals;
Woe to any demon who attempts to enter here.
I am the Protector, guardian of mortals.
I attend the infant when his mother is not near.
Sleep, little *hsiao tzu*, innocent and frail.
Sleep, while I rock your cradle with my tail.
I shall guard the house while watching over you:
Oriental gentleman, T'ien Lung Fu!

16

Song of Shen-lung Po, black four-clawed dragon, who brings the rains:

Thundermaker lizard, masterful and proud,
Flying over mountains in a black and silver cloud.
Feed me tea and ginger roots, and I shall bring the *rain*
. . . for apricots and grain.
See you do not anger me, or I shall bring the *flood*
. . . for pestilence and mud.
Riverkeeper waterlord, master of the flow:
Rain wizard, vain lizard Shen-lung Po!

Triumphal Song of His Imperial Excellency the Lord Most High Lung Wang Hao, golden five-clawed dragon who is very like a god:

From far Kiangsu to the China Sea,
I bring to those who honour me
Peace and pleasure, truth and treasure,
Happiness beyond all measure.
Light the incense, strong and sweet,
For the Dragon-Lord elite.
From high Tibet to old Hankow,
Venerate me: Lung Wang Hao!

The dance of the dragons:

Play the silver bells and blow the golden reeds.
Summon twenty ministers to see to all our needs.
Honour us and we shall bring prosperity to you:
 Lung Wang Hao,
  Shen-lung Po,
   T'ien Lung Fu!

Originally published in *Isaac Asimov's Science Fiction Magazine*, January 1981.

> "The observation of any phenomenon automatically modifies the phenomenon."
> — *Heisenberg's Uncertainty Principle*

Oh, the Heisenberg's plight
Is peculiar, all right;
An extremely grotesque situation.
For he frequently tries
To determine his size
And his colour, shape, form, and location.
But as soon as he checks
His address or his sex
By conducting a brief observation . . .
The parameters change,
And the facts rearrange,
And he undergoes modification.
(If the compass should say
He's in downtown L.A.,
Then he must be in Paddington Station!)

Oh, the Heisenberg's home was constructed in Rome.
(You can see it in Mexico City.)
And to get there he drives to Quebec, and arrives
In southeastern Brazil. (What a pity!)
Now it happens, by chance, that his job is in France.
(Which is why he commutes to Montana.)
But his personal jet (which he flies to Tibet)
Is a boat, and it's bound for Havana!

Oh, the Heisenberg's life is confusing: his wife
Is a blonde-haired brunette known as Karen.
But her name is Diane, so he calls her Suzanne,
And she slaps him and says: "My name's *Sharon!*"
And their afternoon meal (which appears to be veal)
Is a steak, so he finishes carving
And remarks to his mate, heaping food on her plate:
"I've been eating all day, so I'm starving."

Oh, the Heisenberg's world is confusingly twirled,
For the ice-caps are at the Equator.
And the sun sets at noon, for it orbits the moon.
(I'll explain all the harder parts later!)
All the Heisenberg's maps and his data collapse,
And his findings emerge badly shaken;
For as soon as he *knows* how the universe goes
. . . something changes, and then he's mistaken.

Originally published in *Amazing Stories*, March 1984.

The Doppelgänger

In Brompton Road I chanced to see
A man who looked the same as me.
In every wrinkle, trace, and line
His face was just the same as mine.
Our clothes were of the same design;
But *how* can such things be?

The stranger looked up, and *he called me by name,*
And I waited until he came closer.
And he said: "There's a reason that we look the same;
I'll explain it, if you'd care to know, sir.
I have copied your walk, and the way that you talk;
I have stolen your form and your face, sir.
Take my hand! — I insist! — *You will cease to exist,*
You will vanish, *and I'll take your place, sir . . ."*

He reached for me; I turned and fled.
"Come back, young man!" the phantom said.
And as he faded from my view
I heard him say: "I'll follow you;
We'll meet again, and when we do,
Soon after, you'll be dead."

A month has gone by, but I always have known
That some place far away in the distance
Lurks a man with a face *just the same as my own*
And who covets my very existence.
And some day we will meet in some preordained street
And my nightmarish double will face me.
On that terrible day *I shall vanish away*
And the man with my face will replace me . . .

The years have passed; I'm eighty-nine.
My life's at last in dim decline.
These ancient legs are far too sore
For me to travel anymore.
What's this? A man is at the door.
His face looks just like mine . . .

Originally published in *Isaac Asimov's Science Fiction Magazine*, June 1982.

The Bump in the Night

'The Bump in the Night' has special significance for me. I became a professional author in the early 1960s, when a London firm named Badger Books published several crap-awful science-fiction novels which I wrote for them under a house pseudonym. (Those novels were so ruddy awful, I should have written them under a house.) I beavered away on nearly ten years' worth of hackwork before I was willing to put my right name on anything I wrote. Eventually, my work became popular enough for a brave editor named George Scithers to proclaim my contribution to his magazine by *printing my name on the cover*. This was the July 1983 number of *Amazing Stories* . . . which offered the first appearance of my poem *'The Bump in the Night'*, and the first time that my name appeared on the front cover of any publication.

Some people are forever finding Secret Subtexts. Even when an author clearly declares his or her intentions, there will always be a few Deconstructionists (this word is pronounced 'morons') who claim to have discovered the 'true' meaning beneath the author's self-evident words. Several such ~~morons~~ people have claimed to 'know for a fact' that my poem *'The Bump in the Night'* is 'really' about a CAT. They are mistaken. If I had wanted to write a poem about a cat, I would have done so. This poem is titled *'The Bump in the Night'* because it is well and truly a poem about *(wait for it!)* a Bump in the Night. Not cats at all.

However, some people in this world are so cat-besotted that they will spend good money on cat books, cat calendars, cat candles, cat incense, cat wallpaper, cat underwear, cat vibrators, cat cookies, cat thermonuclear generators, and any other sort of merchandise that is remotely related to cats. To *those* people I say: yes, this poem is really about . . . a *CAT!* How very clever of you to figure it out!

There are monsters and creatures and blood-chilling screechers
Of all sizes, shapes and descriptions.
There's a spectre whose shriek can make strong men turn weak
And whose groans can give ladies conniptions.
But the worst one of all, one who makes my flesh crawl,
One who brings me to frenzies of fright
Is that grim serenader, that midnight invader:
The thing that goes BUMP in the night.

For it squats in my bedroom, all shadow and creep,
And goes BUMPETY-BUMP while I'm trying to sleep.
As soon as the sun sets and curtains are drawn
The BUMPing begins, and continues till dawn.
I ask for some quiet, but hard as I try,
BUMP-UMPETY-BUMP is the constant reply.
I threaten, I wheedle, I plead and I sob;
The BUMP keeps BUMP-UMPING, for BUMPing's its job.
(I wish I could turn down the BUMP's volume knob.)

So now — pale, exhausted — I lie here awake
And wish that the BUMP, for variety's sake,
Would make a new noise: *any* noise except BUMP.
Such as CLATTER, or JANGLE, or TINKLE, or THUMP,
Or HI-DIDDLE-DIDDLE, or CLANG, or KERCHOO,
Or SHOO-BOP-A-DOO-WOP-A-BOOP-OOP-A-DOO.
But all the long night, while I lie in a lump,
Comes BUMPETY-BUMP-UMP-A-RUMP-A-TUMP-BUMP!

There are monsters and creatures with horrorsome features
And shapes to drive men to insanity.
There are zombies who munch on cadavers for lunch,
There are demons who dine on humanity.
But I don't care a bit if the poltergeists flit
Or the hobgoblins caper and leap.
I don't mind if they try it, so long as they're *QUIET*
At night, when I'm trying to sleep.

the Kraken

Don't waken the Kraken, whatever you do;
He sleeps in the deeps of the billowing blue.
Take heed; for indeed, what I tell you is true:
You mustn't awaken the Kraken.
The Kraken eats bacon and mulligan stew
And codfish and scrodfish and mackerel too.
And yet I would bet that he'd rather eat *you!*
So please don't awaken the Kraken.

In the far northern regions, the ancient Norwegians
Still speak of the Kraken who plunders their shore:
He rips open ships with his tentacled grips
And he drags sailors down to the dark ocean floor.
No ship can escape him (though many have tried)
For his jaws are so wide *twenty men* fit inside,
And he chuckles with pride just to think how they died.
A terrible sea-myth,
    A monstrous behemoth;
        He travels from Norway
            To distant Land's End.
                (If he's coming *your* way
                    You've had it, my friend.)

The Kraken has taken a very dim view
Of sailors and whalers; he's gobbled a few.
He'll eat up a fleet and he'll chew on the crew.
So *please* don't awaken the Kraken!
The Kraken, forsaken, befriended by few,
Stays home in the foam of the bottomless blue.
He's lonely; if only some circus or zoo
Would offer to take in the Kraken!

With cool calculation the Kraken pretends
He *can't* understand why he never makes friends.
Yet deep down inside, he is fully aware
Of *why* people never come visit his lair:
It isn't his looks, and it can't be his breath.
Nor is it his handshake (a fate worse than death);
It's just that — when somebody visits — he meets them,
And greets them, and treats them, and seats them
. . . and *eats* them.
(The shipwreck that happened last week? I've a hunch
The crewmen wound up as a Krakenous lunch.)

Come all ye bold sailors, ye captains and crew.
Beware of the Kraken: he's looking for *you*.
Don't sleep while on duty, because if you do
You might just awake in
The Kraken.

Originally published in *Amazing Stories*, September 1986.

THE HOLLOW
EARTHERS

The Earth has holes at both its poles,
And in the land between them
There dwells a race from Inner Space
(No mortal man has seen them).
In grim patrols they guard their holes
And let no humans enter;
Like ghastly trolls, bereft of souls,
They lurk in Terra's center.

Beware the Hollow-Earthers! Beware the troglodytes!
They make their homes in catacombs, and prowl on moonless nights . . .
They kidnap helpless children, they steal the babes at birth
And make them slaves inside the caves of hellish Hollow-Earth . . .

No man who's faced the Arctic waste
And fought the savage frost there
Has found the hole beneath the Pole.
(God help the man who's *lost* there!)
The Eskimos claim no-one knows
The tunnel's point of entry.
And yet they swear the hole is *there*,
Complete with loathsome sentry.

Beware the Hollow-Earthers! They dwell in lumps of clay!
Like fiendish moles they leave their holes and stalk their human prey . . .
Don't let them know you're out there! Run home for all you're worth!
Take care to flee if you should see the fiends from Hollow-Earth . . .

Some hardy soul must reach the Pole
(Equipped with charts and data)
And find, up there, the creatures' lair
Beneath the polar strata.
Some day, no doubt, we'll rout them out
By ending our reliance
On ancient myth, and siding with
The tools of modern science.

Destroy the Hollow-Earthers! Let nightmares melt away!
Like motes of dust, it seems they must avoid the light of day!
Avoid such fiends in future, and grant them wider berth . . .
I'd rather see reality; who needs a Hollow-Earth?

Political Correctness Alert
(Danger! Danger! Warning! Warning!)

I have received a letter from some Trendy Liberals who
object to my use of the word 'Eskimos' in this poem.
Apparently the Arctic's inhabitants, popularly known as
Eskimos or — worse luck — *Esquimaux*, prefer to be known
as the Yupik, Inupiat, Gwichin and Inuit peoples. For the
benefit of readers who are Eskimophobic, therefore, I say:
Yupik another name; I can't get Inuit.

Originally published in *Isaac Asimov's Science Fiction Magazine*, February 1982.

The

The Clone, the Clone is never alone
— a fact which the Clone has been known to bemoan —
For research in biogenetics has shown
That Clones always come from a Cloner.
Now birds and bees (the drones and the queens)
Develop their genes by the usual means
(As Mendel has proven with peas and with beans),
But Clones get their genes from a donor.

"Good gosh!" said a Clone named Tryone with a groan,
As he swallowed two aspirins and picked up the phone,
"I'm giving a party next Saturday night;
I've ordered the food and libations.
But now comes the hard part: I have to invite
My nearest and dearest relations.
I've a father, a mother, two sisters, a brother;
They're all in my family tree.
And Clones by the dozens are nephews and cousins,
But all my relations are *ME!*
I was twinned from myself on a scientist's shelf
(That's a fact upon which I do pride myself.)
But if he, she, and we are just copies of *me*
I'll get so mad I'll be, well, *beside* myself!"

The Clone, the Clone is easily grown:
He's partially muscle and partially bone,
And into a beaker he's frequently thrown
By some biologic mechanic.
Now birds and bees (the queens and the drones)
Make excellent subjects to turn into Clones.
But don't waste your time making Clones out of *stones*,
For stones are so seldom organic.

Now the Clone named Tyrone met a Clone name of Joan,
And they married without any fuss.
But Tyrone said: "Now maybe, if we have a baby,
He might just turn out to be *US!*
Let me see, now: if I
Take the chromosome Y
And I change it to chromosome X
(Which I cannot condone)
The result is a Clone
Who would be of the opposite sex!"

The Clone, the Clone is never alone,
But if he were flown to some faraway zone
The Clone might develop a life all his own
(And not merely copy another).
The Clone, you see, can never agree
On where he should be in his family tree;
He'll never be certain he really is *HE*
And not, for example, his brother.

☞ Moral: ☜

If you can't find your chromosomes, try looking in your other set of genes.

Originally published in *Isaac Asimov's Science Fiction Magazine*, September 1981.

THE VAMPIRE

Robots get rusty and Ghouls smell revolting.
Werewolves are musty and Harpies keep moulting.
In all the array of the damned and the doomed,
The Vampire alone is impeccably groomed.
Trolls are disgusting and Goblins are grimy.
Mummies want dusting and Swamp Things are slimy.
Of all the undead and the dread and depraved,
The Vampire alone is well-bred and behaved.

His cape is black satin, his bearing is suave.
His blood-lines are Latin, his accent is Slav.
He casts no rude shadow, he throws no reflection;
The Vampire's as regal and proud as the Sphinx.
His manners (while drinking your blood) are perfection;
He makes you feel *glad* to get stuck for the drinks!
When choosing a victim, he first stops to check . . .
And says "Pardon my fangs; may I *please* bite your neck?"

Man-Eating Plants tend to play with their food.
Huge Mutant Ants are inclined to be rude.
Unlike all the other unnatural terrors,
The Vampire alone doesn't show up in mirrors.
Sentient Fungoids are frequently rotting.
Blood-Sucking Zombies are constantly clotting.
Of all the perverse and profoundly profane,
The Vampire keeps going all night . . . in this vein.

Originally published in *Worlds of Fantasy & Horror*, Summer 1994.

The NIGHTMARE

When I am alone, then the Nightmare comes . . .
Introducing itself with a grin.
It bestraddles my head, and persistently drums
On my skull, while it shrieks: *"Let me in!"*
It unfastens the latch on the doors of my mind —
It steps over the threshold, its glee unconfined —
And it drags several sinister satchels behind
As it props up its feet on my brain.
Then I ask why it sits, tucked away in my wits,
And the Nightmare replies: *"You're insane."*

When I am in crowds, then the Nightmare broods . . .
And it whispers dark thoughts in my ear.
And no person who looks at me ever concludes
I am other than as I appear.
But the Nightmare has secretly taken control
Of my voice and my body, my thoughts and my soul;
It unbuckles my flesh, and it swallows me whole,
Then it tries on my body for size.
And the man people see — whom they fancy is *me* —
Is the Nightmare in human disguise.

When I am asleep, then the Nightmare rides
Through a dark and foreboding terrain.
And the alien shores of the land it explores
Are the valleys and shoals of my brain.
And the Nightmare wears faces I don't want to see;
It pursues me eternally, howling with glee,
And it traps me in realms where I never can flee
From the Nightmare within, which inhabits my skin.
And before I can ask
   Why its face is concealed
      By a hideous mask,
         All at once it's revealed:
And the form of the Nightmare has steadily grown
To resemble myself . . . *and its face is my own.*

Originally published in *Weird Tales*, Fall 1989.

The Gremlin and the Glitch

On the shores of space, at the Earthfleet base,
When the starships yaw and pitch
There are beasts, no doubt, you will hear about
Called the Gremlin and the Glitch.
When the proton force blows a ship off-course
And the ion motors twitch
All the spacemen claim you can place the blame
On the Gremlin and the Glitch.

For the Gremlin plays with the cosmic rays
In the depths of a nebula cloud,
And she shoots croquet with the Milky Way,
And the universe laughs out loud.
So when spacemen roam far away from home,
And their gravity fields grow weak,
Or their photon rays travel out of phase,
Or the coffee pot springs a leak,
Or if something goes wrong, well, it doesn't take long
To determine who gets the blame:
But you'll never find a trace of that critter from space
. . . and the *Gremlin* is her name!

If an engine appears to be stripping its gears
And it makes strange noises and hums . . .
If a data bank chooses to blow twenty fuses
When it should be counting up sums . . .

If the captain's spare pants just get up and dance,
While the robots twiddle their thumbs . . .
Or if anything breaks or falls apart,
The spacemen nod and look real smart
And the new recruits will find
That they have signed
Up for a hitch
On a starship that's bedeviled
By the Gremlin and the Glitch!

Now the Glitch plays pranks with oxygen tanks,
And he bollixes machines.
And the Glitch just smiles when atomic piles
Get blown to smithereens.
So if something goes wrong on your trip to the stars —
If you aim for Jupiter but land on Mars —
If your problems never go away,
Then you can bet some niche
Of your spaceship has a stowaway:
The grinning, gleeful *Glitch!*

Moral:

So when that pair of holy terrors
(Who delight in causing errors
And who make machines malfunction)
Try to come and bother *you,*
Then the only thing to do
Is to QWERTYUIOP ETAOIN SHRDLU SHRDLU SHRDLU

Note: Due to a sudden inexplicable malfunction
inside our brand-new high-tech digital laser ink-jet
phototype printing mainframe, we regret to inform
you that PYRZQXGL EFSITZ IRTNOG.

Originally published in *Isaac Asimov's Science Fiction Magazine*, August 1981.

The frumious Bandersnatch, as everyone must know by now, was created by Lewis Carroll for his epic poem *'Jabberwocky'*. Unfortunately, Carroll neglected to tell us what a Bandersnatch actually *is* . . . and why they are so frumious. In the following poem, I have humbly attempted to address that lapse.

The Bandersnatch*

*(frumius carrollii)

You cannot catch a Bandersnatch with cages, traps or snares,
Or nooses, knots, or lobster-pots or other such affairs.
The plan you need that's guaranteed to lure them from their lairs —
To catch a batch of Bandersnatches — catch them UNAWARES!

Any physicist would lack words to explain how this takes place,
But the Bandersnatch goes *backwards* relative to Time and Space.
From the Future, its location changes yesterwards so fast
That its final destination is three Tuesdays in the past.
Thus the Bandersnatch migration is a strange phenomenon:
It arrives before it gets there, and it leaves before it's gone!

You cannot match the Bandersnatch for doing what it doesn't;
It hides behind the yesterdays and pops out where it wasn't.
You cannot catch the Bandersnatch with handcuffs, badge, or warrant
Unless you know a way to go and meet it where you aren't.

Bandersnatches may astound one; all the same, I must insist
That the fact nobody's found one is the proof that they exist!
You may sneak up right behind one, but it's gone before you've blinked.
Ah, but if you ever *find* one . . . well, that proves it: they're extinct.

Originally published in *Amazing Stories*, November 1987.

The Other

If life is a banquet, I wasn't invited.
And yet uninvited I nonetheless came.
The feast was prepared, and the music delighted;
'Tis pity the guest-list excluded my name.
The laughter grew loud whilst the revels increased,
Yet I hungered while gentlemen ate.
For I am the Other, ignored at the feast.
And I watch in the dark, and I wait . . .

The music runs faster, the revelries flourish,
The ladies sup wine till their bodices burst.
And where in this feast is the food that will nourish
My hunger? The drink that will silence my thirst?
No guest in this hall — not the first, nor the least —
Deigns to spare me a crust from his plate.
For I am the Other, who starves at the feast.
And I watch in the dark, and I wait . . .

And now there is silence, the dancers grow cold
And the wine lingers warm in the cask.
On the table are goblets of crystal and gold;
I ignore them, and bend to my task.
The hunger within me at last is released
In this harlequinade of the dead.
For I am the Other, who came to the feast.
And I waited, and watched . . . *and I fed.*

Originally published in *Worlds of Fantasy & Horror*, Summer 1994.

The BLOB

Oh, it fell from the sky on a night in July;
Its arrival was quite surreptitious.
It began as a speck of mysterious dreck,
But it proved itself highly ambitious.
For it turned into goo which resembled a brew
Made of gelatin, glue, and a leftover stew —
And it grew and it *grew* and it GREW and it *GREW*
Till it swallowed six cows and a farmer or two,
Smacked its lips, and exclaimed *"How delicious!"*

Oh, it came up the street seeking something to eat,
But the townspeople saw the Blob coming.
Well, they bolted the doors and plugged up all the floors,
But the Blob came right in through the plumbing.
All the people it met were extremely upset
To be eaten like so many pickles.
Lots of children were screaming (and likewise adults)
When along came the scientist Ludwig von Schultz.
"I can kill it," he said, "and I promise results!"
Then he blasted the Blob with a few billion volts
But the Blob just replied "Hey, that *tickles!*"

Oh, we stared in surprise while it doubled in size;
Now the Blob was so big it could dwarf us.
"We're doomed!" someone cried. "Now the Blob's a mile wide,
And besides that . . . it's all *polymorphous!*"
There were shouts of disorder and *"Head for the border*
Before that big Blob tries to flatten us!
It's a gluttonous, glutinous, thoroughly mutinous
Blob that's completely GELATINOUS!"

Oh, the Blob shook like Jell-O, turned orange and yellow,
And polka-dot plaid polychromic.
Then it headed northeast, chomping human and beast,
While it ate its way up the Potomac.
It digested its fill up on Capitol Hill;
There was clearly no way to appease it.
Then a kid in the crowd shouted out very loud:
"We can stop the Blob now if we *freeze it!"*

Well, we ended the slaughter with sprays of ice water;
The Blob never knew we'd defeat it.
Now we keep it ice-cold in a gelatin mold,
And as soon as it's frozen . . . we'll *eat it!*
Everyone gets a slice of the Blob served on ice.
(Say, it's not too much work for the chef, is it?)
When it's frozen this way, the Blob makes a *parfait*
That's as big as the federal deficit.

Originally published in *Weird Tales*, Summer 1991.

THE POOKAH

A bold Irish spook, a weird beast is the Pookah:
The mischievous imp of indefinite shape.
And if by some fluke a pestiferous Pookah
Should latch on to *you* there's no chance of escape.
The Pookah resembles a hound or a hare,
An ox or a fox or a boar or a bear.
The prank-loving Pookah seeks fun; nothing more.
So never insult him, or else . . . he'll get *sore!*
And any palooka who tries to rebuke a
Pestiferous Pookah gets trouble galore!

Though Celtic by nature and Irish by birth,
The Pookah's been sighted all over the Earth.
Reliable sources have spotted the Pookah
In Upper Zambezi and downtown Paducah.
A huge hairy Pookah, for reasons quite strange,
Invaded the U.S. Marines' target range.
"Destroy it!" the general screeched to his aides.
"Use pistols! Use rifles! Use rocket grenades!
Unleash the commandos, and fetch my bazooka!
Declare total war! But *get rid of that Pookah!"*
A joint Army-Navy-Marine exercise
Fired howitzer shells and rained death from the skies.
But when the dust settled, and then came the dawn:
"When's breakfast?" the Pookah remarked with a yawn.

Originally published in *Weird Tales*, Summer 1990.

A soldier named Duke (a John Wayne type of hero)
Said "Let's blast the Pookah; we'll make him Ground Zero."
And thus was constructed, with grace and aplomb,
A ninety-five megaton hydrogen bomb.
The bomber crew dropped its unstoppable load
On the spot where the Pookah relaxed in the road.
And then came a flash; the whole neighborhood glowed
While the Pookah-bomb's atoms began to *explode!*

And when it was over . . . there, in his peruke — a
Small wig that he wore — yes, and smoking a hookah,
And daintily sipping a glass of *Sambouca*
While strumming a uke . . . ah, you've guessed it: *the Pookah!*
And thus was established what none can deny:
You can't nuke a Pookah, so don't even try.

'The Pookah' (which was nominated for the 1990 Rhysling Award by the Science Fiction Poetry Association) came to me in an unusual way. By the late 1980s, most of the best-known mythological beasties had already been included in my **Improbable Bestiary**, and I had to stretch my brain a bit (always a nasty business, that) in order to think of crypto-critters who might be fresh candidates for my muse.

On 14 November 1988, at the Shubert Theatre in New York City, I attended a memorial celebration in honour of the great Broadway director Joshua Logan. Among the speakers that day was the actor James Stewart, who had known Logan since their days together at Princeton. While Stewart spoke, I recalled that he had starred in the film version (and several stage productions) of **Harvey**, the Pulitzer Prize-winning play about a man who has his own personal pookah. Right there and then in the Shubert Theatre, while Stewart stood onstage reminiscing about Logan, I sat amidst the audience: listening to Stewart with half of my brain, whilst the other half composed the poem which you see here.

As for those dark circular objects which randomly festoon this page . . . well, those are pookah dots.

The Invisible Man

I never have seen an Invisible Man.
(In fact, I don't see how I possibly *can!*)
And if *you* see Invisible Men, I surmise
There is probably something quite wrong with your eyes.
Invisible Men — if you see what I mean —
Can never be, ever be *possibly* seen.
If you *see* an Invisible Man, I would swear
That to see him would prove that *he's not really there!*
But if *no* Invisible Men should appear,
The fact you don't see them *is proof that they're here!*
(I hope that I'm making this perfectly clear.)

The Invisible Man periodically tries
To materialize in a visible guise.
He dresses himself in some visible clothes,
Then he puts on dark glasses, a pink plastic nose,
And bandages — usually *plenty* of those!
And when asked, "Why the bandages, bub?" he explains:
"Don't you know who you're speaking to, sir? I'm Claude Rains."

There's no cure for the poor old Invisible Man;
When he goes to the seashore, he can't get a tan.
The people who meet him can never tell *where*
His neck culminates in his head and his hair.
(He went to a barber and asked for a shave,
And wound up instead with a permanent wave.)

This poem was originally published in *Isaac Asimov's Science Fiction Magazine*, February 1983 ... which explains the reference to 'this very fine magazine'.

The Invisible Man's not as shy as you'd think;
For he wrote me a note (with invisible ink)
Which said: "I've consented — that is, I agree —
To come out of hiding. Just pay a small fee
And I'll send you a photo I recently took,
So all of your readers can see how I look."

Yes, now the Invisible Man can be *seen!*
In the pages of this very fine magazine
In accord with our editor's plan.
So come on, then, let's go: in the photo below
We present . . .

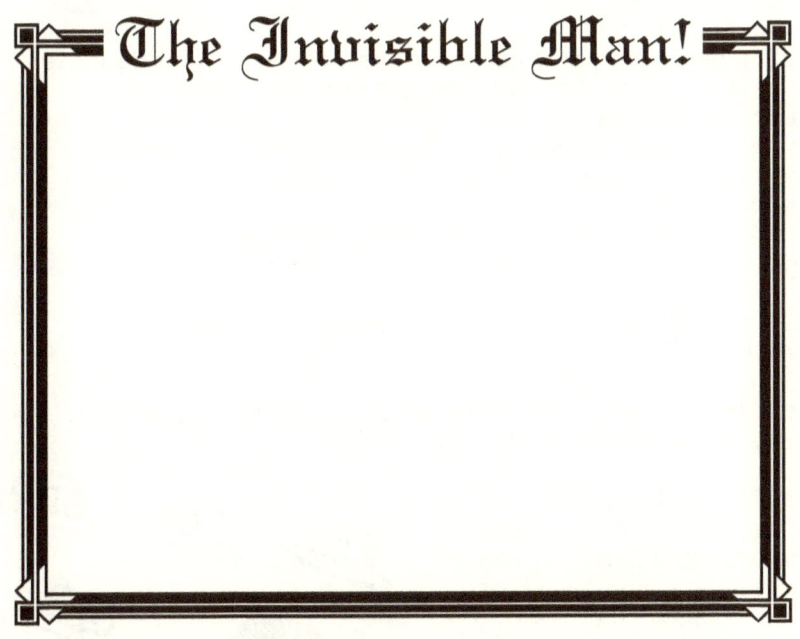

The Invisible Man!

Memo from F. Gwynplaine MacIntyre to Editor:
As promised, I enclose a photograph of the
Invisible Man. Please send payment for same.

Reply from Editor to F. Gwynplaine MacIntyre:
We have received your Invisible Man photo. It is
the best Invisible Man photo that we have ever seen
(also the clearest), and we intend to publish it.
The payment will be DOUBLE our usual rate.
We enclose an invisible check.

The Little Green Men

Oh, we came from outer space
To destroy the human race,
And we'll battle face-to-face
With some eccentric scientist.
Then we'll pillage, loot, and slaughter everyone except his daughter
Though of course (because we've caught her)
She will struggle and resist.
So we'll throw a rope across her and we'll tie her up and toss her
In a waiting flying saucer
And take off without delay.
Back on Mars a little later, the Galactic High Dictator
Will begin his plan to *mate* her, so she'll scream and run away!

We attack and loot and sack and shoot disintegrator guns,
And every human runs
Except (of course) the ones
We snatch and nab and catch and grab and capture for the Fleet.
And then we take 'em back to Mars and *EAT!*

Every day for lunch we feed
On Earthlings fried and fricasseed,
Earthling soup and Earthling roast,
Earthling finely chopped on toast.
Then, for dinner, we'll unleash
Plans to dine on Earthling *quiche!*
(Of all the species we have faced,
Earthlings have the nicest taste.)

Our photon guns will flatten
Half the buildings in Manhattan;
All the planets we've attacked like this
Have shattered, one by one.
And we'll have such jolly games
As the Earth explodes in flames.
Ever wonder why we *act* like this?
Because it's lots of *fun!*

Originally published in *Amazing Stories*, November 1985.

The Unicorn

Now, once there was a unicorn, and she was very sad.
Her forehead bore a single horn and that was all she had.
She knew that gnu and caribou have horns that come in sets of *two*
But poor old unicorns make do with just one horn. Too bad!

And then she met a scientist, a young and handsome scientist
Who said to her: "I'll change you into anything you say.
You want *two* horns? Why, that's a breeze!
I'll make them any shape you please!
And all I have to do is recombine your DNA."

He figured out some calculus, a secant and a sine.
He multiplied the answer by the cubic root of nine.
And then her horn turned green and blue
And changed, transmogrified, and grew
Until at last it split in TWO! *"Two* horns!" she gasped. "That's fine!"

"You're welcome," said the scientist (a Nobel Prize geneticist).
"I'm glad my calculations worked according to the plan.
And if there's more that you require — or anything that you desire —
Just let me know, and I'll help out in any way I can."

The one-horned unicorns came by, too numerous by half.
"A *two*-horned unicorn!" they sneered. "You look like a giraffe!"
But then, when she began to speak, and said: "I'm really quite unique . . ."
They scoffed: *"The word for you is* FREAK!*"* And they began to laugh . . .

The scientist then quickly went to his two-horned experiment
And said: "I'll make you look like them as easy as can be."
"Not bloody likely, chum!" she cried. "I'm *not* like them!" she said with pride.
"Who wants to be like everybody else?" she said. "NOT *ME!"*

The one-horned unicorns all laughed at her and nudged and winked
. . . and three days later one-horned unicorns became extinct.
Our two-horned friend is still unique; she rides the plains of Mozambique
And lives with a romantic sheik who feeds her sweetmeats every week
And never, *never* calls her "freak" . . . and every night they dance.
And her scientist friend did all right in the end:
He received twelve government grants.

Originally published in *Isaac Asimov's Science Fiction Magazine*, April 1981.

I wrote 'The Missing Link' in 1981, when the airwaves over America (and, to a lesser extent, Britain) struggled under the weight of a broadcast called 'The Tonight Show' featuring a singularly smug and self-satisfied *compère* named Johnny Carson. Thus, this poem contains a reference to 'Carson's "Tonight Show"'.

Future generations will have forgotten Johnny Carson altogether, so I was tempted to expunge him from this poem. But then I recalled two similar examples. One of Lewis Carroll's poems in **Through the Looking-Glass** contains a reference to Rowland's Macassar Oil: this was a genuine brand-name product (a scented hair oil) that was popular in Victorian England but which no longer exists. Carroll's poem is still funny anyway. Ira Gershwin's song lyric 'But Not for Me' — written in 1929 — contains a reference to one Beatrice Fairfax: an advice columnist (of the sort known in Britain as an 'agony aunt') who would now be entirely forgotten . . . if not for the fact that Ira Gershwin mentioned her in his song. Miss Fairfax's name continues to be heard (and sung) by future generations . . . but *only* because the Ira Gershwin song which mentions her is still popular.

So, who knows? In the year 2375, Johnny Carson may well have vanished entirely into the mists of oblivion . . . *except* for the fact that he was once mentioned in one of my poems.

THE Missing Link

I do not think the Missing Link
Will ever take up pen and ink
And sign an agreement which says that he *might* show
Himself to the crowd at a rock concert light-show.
(I *know* he's not slated for Carson's "Tonight Show"!)
A whimsical loner is he.
He'll refuse to embark on a show-biz career;
You can offer him pretzels and offer him beer,
And say "please" on your knees for the rest of the year.
You can book him in Vegas; he'll never come near,
And he'll *never* be seen on TV. . .
For if he should appear on a show, then I fear
That he wouldn't be Missing, you see.

I do not think the Missing Link
Is polka-dot or striped or pink
Or two-tone magenta, or purple, or puce;
I know for a *fact* that he isn't chartreuse!
Or green, tangerine, or . . . oh, heck: What's the use?
It might even be that he's *plaid!*
He avoids all the sculptors who ask him to pose
And the agents who promise to publish his prose,
And he flees from the pleas and entreaties of those
Who wave Kodaks and tell him to take off his clothes.
And he *never* has guests, I might add . . .
For if he should disclose where he lives, I suppose
That he wouldn't be Missing, by gad.

BEAM ME UP, SCOTTY: On rare occasions throughout my work
— such as here in *'The Missing Link'* and in my poem *'The Blob'* —
I've used the word 'plaid' to indicate a certain pattern of colours, like
the intersecting stripes woven into a Scotsman's kilt. I have only ever
used this term when writing in American publications for American
readers. In the United States, this sort of pattern is indeed known
as 'plaid'.

However, as a proud Scotsman — and occasional kilt-wearer —
I am fully aware that the pattern in a Scotsman's kilt is correctly
known as a *tartan*. The word *plaid* correctly denotes the woven fabric
itself, not the pattern of colours.

During my young and scuffling days, after I left Australia and
returned to my native Scotland, I briefly found employment as a
brickie (a construction worker) in the Clydeside dockyards. My first
day on the job, the foreman sent me off the worksite to fetch some
tartan paint . . . a paint which leaves a *plaid* pattern. This was,
of course, an initiation ritual. I might have done worse: one of my
workmates was sent to fetch a bubble for a spirit level.

So dinnae ye fash yersel', and please don't send me any letters
claiming that I dinnae ken the difference between plaid and tartan.
Now, if you'll excuse me, the boss wants me to bring him a
three-handed pickaxe. Och aye!

Originally published in *Isaac Asimov's Science Fiction Magazine*, October 1981.

THE BIGFOOT

While thrashing about in the Oregon woods
(And my haversack filled overflowing
With camping equipment, provisions and goods)
I lost track of which way I was going.
With no rescue in sight, I made camp for the night,
Pitched a tent and ignited a fire.
And then in the dark I was startled to see
A huge hairy creature as tall as a tree.
"Hello there," he rumbled, *"I happen to be
Mister Bigfoot J. Sasquatch, Esquire."*

"Folks would pay through the nose for a look at those toes,"
I remarked, when I saw his huge footsies.
"With your feet on display we'll get rich right away,
Showing off your miraculous tootsies.
I know just what to do; come with me to the zoo!
Have you got any brothers or sisters?"
"I can't go into town!" Bigfoot roared with a frown.
"For the streets give my poor old feet blisters!"

"I've twenty-six bunions the size of spring onions,"
The Bigfoot explained, "and my toes are so sore.
The sidewalks have got holes, the highways have potholes;
The street hurts my feet, as I mentioned before."
"Don't worry," I said, while the tears filled his eyes.
"I'll treat your poor feet with my camping supplies.
I have here two war-surplus hammocks, for starters;
On legs of *your* size, they'd make excellent garters.
To save your poor feet from the harsh pavement's shocks,
These two sleeping-bags will make excellent socks.
And now you'll need shoes; I know just what to use:
Stick your feet in these extra-large birchbark canoes.
Try 'em on," I remarked. "If your feet like the fit,
You can walk twenty miles without hurting a bit."

So Bigfoot J. Sasquatch, not skipping a beat,
Quite rapidly garbed his voluminous feet.
"THEY FIT!" he exclaimed. *"Life is nearly complete!
All I need now is LOTS OF NICE HUMANS TO EAT!"*
Then he hightailed it off towards the city.
Where's he *now?* Need you *ask?* Watch
Out, folks; Mister Sasquatch
Is heading *your* way . . . what a pity.

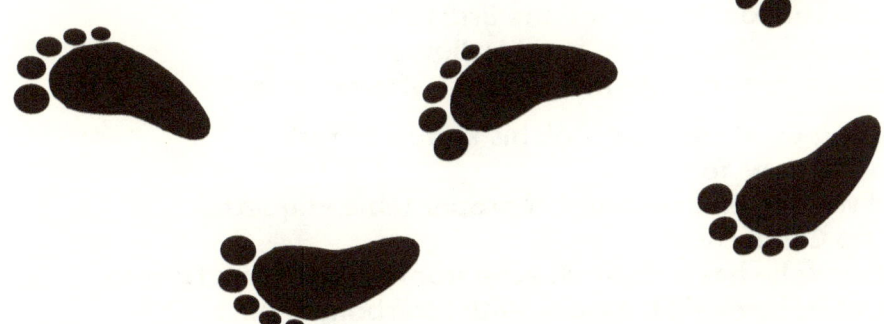

Originally published in *Weird Tales*, Spring 1988.

45

THE BUG-EYED MONSTER

The Bug-Eyed Monster eats virgins for lunch;
He likes to hear their bones going crunch, crunch, crunch.
He has twelve arms and sixteen legs,
His breath smells just like rotten eggs,
His face is so ugly it *must* be a curse . . .
And those are his *good* points; from here it gets worse.

The Bug-Eyed Monster round our street
Has sixteen ugly, hairy feet.
(And it's *not* very nice to make fun of them!)
The Bug-Eyed Monster round our street
Has *tons* of things he loves to eat.
(And humans, he tells me, are one of them.)
The local Bug-Eyed Monster is a notable gourmet.
Last night he ate three lamp posts and a two-door Chevrolet.
He ate ten thousand loaves of bread; he wasn't getting thinner.
"Well, that's enough for *lunch!*" he said.
"What time shall we have *dinner?*"

Constable Brown came up from town to catch him and arrest him.
The monster saw the constable and started to digest him.
I rung up Sergeant Cripps and brought the matter to his attention.
"If the constable's dead," the sergeant said,
"We won't have to give him his pension."

The Bug-Eyed Monster, without hesitation,
Took pepper and salt and ate Waterloo Station.
He ate Covent Garden. (You really should *see* him!)
He ate London Bridge and the British Museum.
He drank half an ocean, and swallowed a sea.
"Nice dinner!" he told me. "When's afternoon tea?"

The Bug-Eyed Monster took his knife and fork
And ate New York.
And when I reminded him of proper table etiquette
He ate Connecticut.
And now he has a stomach ache from eating North Dakota.
Quick! Help me fill Lake Erie with bicarbonate of soda!

Originally published in *Isaac Asimov's Science Fiction Magazine*, February 1981.

The Time Traveller

Come on right in and we'll begin while I adjust the screen.
For I'm the Chronic Argonaut, and here's my Time Machine.
Just choose a place in Time or Space (or somewhere in between)
Sit back, and then we'll go *Somewhen* inside my Time Machine!

Pick an era to suit yourself: visit your future self.
See ancient Rome in its glory.
You can breakfast with cave-folks, or fly with the brave folks
Who ride the first ship to Centauri.
You can witness the flight of those brothers named Wright,
You can fight an extinct carnivore.
And enlist and enlist and enlist and enlist and enlist in the Hundred Years' War.

Come on right in and we'll begin while I adjust the screen. *(Wait a minute.
I've said that already, haven't I?)*
For I'm the Chronic Argonaut, and here's my Time Machine. *(Aha! Here's the
problem: we're stuck in a closed-loop continuum, and Time is repeating itself.)*
Just choose a place in Time or Space or Time or Space or Time or Space or
Time or Space or (Hmm, the time-stream appears to be doubling back on itself.
Hand me that wrench and stand back, won't you?) Time or Space or Time or
Space or . . . **WHACK!**
Ah, that's better. Now, which time-stream are we *in?*

We'll have lunch with Rasputin and Sir Isaac Newton
While sailing aboard the *Titanic.*
We'll have dinner at one with Attila the Hun
In the midst of the Stock Market Panic.
We'll eat Dinosaur pie and a Dodo on rye
While the maidens of Babylon serve us.
(I've been told Jack the Ripper is quite a good tipper,
But makes all the waitresses nervous.)

Come down the hatch and close the latch while I turn back the clocks.
We're off to reach Infinity; next stop is Paradox!
If anyone wants the Renaissance or the early Pleistocene
Or Ten Million A.D., they can travel with me inside my Time Machine!

Originally published in *Isaac Asimov's Science Fiction Magazine*, September 1983.

Now we come to 'The Elf', which was originally published in the July 1984 number of *Amazing Stories*. Shortly after this poem was published, something rather embarrassing happened . . . which I shall reveal *after* you've read the poem. Here it is:

Way deep in the woods, on a moss-covered shelf
I saw a man one-tenth the size of myself.
"Who are you?" I asked, and he said: *"I'm an Elf!*
With long pointed ears and a cap.
I frolic with moonbeams and sing to the trees,
I float with the butterflies, dance with the breeze . . ."
"Get lost!" I replied. "Could you knock it off, please,
With that moonbeam-and-butterfly crap?"

"I breakfast on dewdrops," he said, *"and I make*
My lunch out of lilacs and gossamer-cake."
"Too bad you don't choke," I said. "Give me a break!
Or do me a favor: go jump in the lake!"
But the Elf said: *"I ride on a dandelion-puff,*
And I flutter, so lively and quick . . ."
"That's enough!" I replied. "Put a lid on that stuff;
You're so cute that I think I'll be sick!"

The Elf said: *"I know how the daffodils grow,*
And I know why the katydids chirp.
And the mystical ways of the Pixies and Fays . . ."
"Shut your trap!" I explained. "You're a twerp!"

But the Elf only smiled like an innocent child
As he scrambled about in the thickets,
And he gathered the notes from the hummingbirds' throats
And collected the songs of the crickets.
And I could not ignore all the mystical lore
And the magical secrets he'd mastered.
But the Elf looked so cute that I lifted my boot
And I *stepped on* the wee little bastard.

Immediately 'The Elf' was published, the editorial offices of *Amazing Stories* were deluged with letters from readers . . . all of them informing us that, several decades earlier, an American poet named Morris Bishop had published a poem bearing the same title as mine. Further, Morris Bishop's poem 'The Elf' and my own effort had some strong similarities. Both poems featured a human narrator with a low tolerance for cute li'l elves. Both poems end with the narrator stomping on the elf. Several readers helpfully enclosed a copy of Morris Bishop's poem with their letters, so that *Amazing*'s editors could see how closely my poem resembled his opus.

In my own defence, I must point out that my own poem has a rhyme scheme and metre which are entirely different from Bishop's poem (which I shan't reprint here). Not a single phrase in my poem resembles any phrase in Bishop's. As for the similar endings, evidently Bishop and I are in agreement on one point: namely, that the only way to deal with cute li'l elves is to stomp their cute li'l butts. When I wrote my own poem 'The Elf', I had never heard of Morris Bishop — much less read any of his work — and the semblance between our two verses was purely a coincidence.

I have always accepted that an author can learn from his (or her) readers, and that my readers know more than I do about a good many subjects. Nonetheless, I was gobsmacked to discover that dozens of *Amazing*'s readers were intimately familiar with the work of a poet who was entirely unknown to *me*. As a result of *l'affaire Elf*, I have been provoked to find and read the collected verses of Morris Bishop. They are excellent. Had I not written 'The Elf', I very likely never would have learnt about Bishop's work. This is one more of the many reasons why I am deeply indebted to my readers.

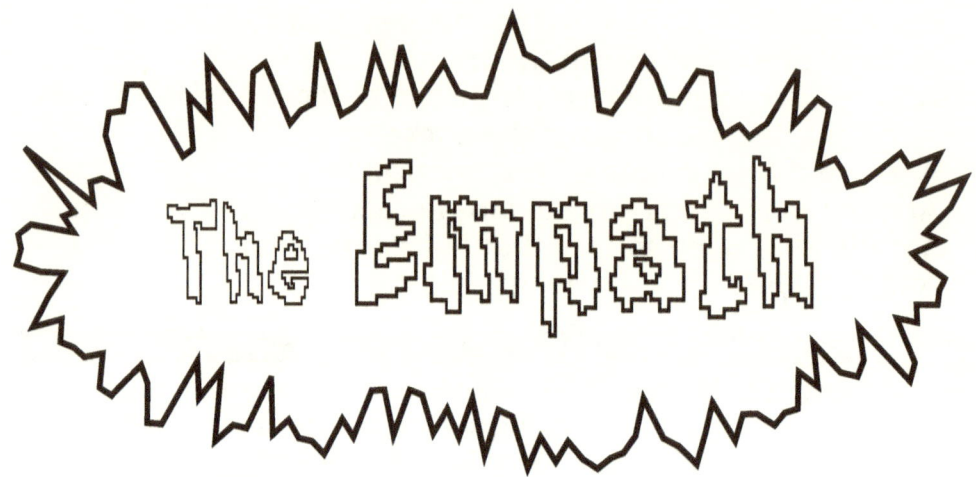

The Empath

They touch my mind: the yearning ones, the ever-discontented ones.
Each thought invades the barricades and borders of my mind.
I feel their thoughts: the burning ones, the howling and demented ones,
The fever-dreams and shattered screams, the lost and the maligned.

I've prayed that they would fade away, but thoughts from everywhere
Invade my head with sorrow, dread, and anger and despair.
I try to hide, I've died inside; the thoughts become a din.
The nightmares find my weary mind and force their way within.
They *touch* my mind, and *clutch* my mind, until the pain is *such* my mind
Will burst, explode, or overload, for I was cursed from birth:
No matter who invents the thoughts,
No matter how intense the thoughts,
God help me, I can sense the thoughts of everyone on Earth!

Some thoughts I sense are pleasant ones, infrequently surrounding me;
Brief interludes of tranquil moods and attitudes of cheer.
But still the ever-present ones, the thoughts forever hounding me
Are panic, grief, and disbelief and agony and *fear*.
The screams of all humanity come clawing at my brain
With chaos and insanity and never-ending pain.
And yet one question stays unclear, one answer still unsaid:
When I die, will I start to hear the nightmares of the dead?

Originally published in *Amazing Stories*, November 1985.

Of all the weird creatures inhabiting my Bestiary, *'The Ghoul'* is the only one of these poems that I've written *while eating a meal.* Which, as you're about to discover, may be ghoulishly appropriate.

The Ghoul, as a rule, is unlikely to drool
Over puddings or porridge or gravy or gruel.
His diet is strict, his reserve never softens:
The meats that he eats must come *packaged in coffins!*
The meals that he steals may be short, tall, or hairy:
Their flavours may change, and their colourings vary,
But nothing will *ever* go down his œsophagus
Unless it's been kept in a tasteful sarcophagus
(He's quite anthropophagous.)

The Ghoul, as a rule, is impassive and cool
Over raspberry trifle and gooseberry fool.
For only one menu can nourish his avarice:
The stews that he chews must be freshly cadaverous!
And this leads to one other delicate matter,
Regarding the Ghoul and the lunch on his platter:

Although he's a glutton, he never steals mutton.
Although he's a thief, he will never take beef.
He'll never be found to impound a ground round,
And he won't even purloin a sirloin.
He's now coming closer; he's
Dragging his groceries
Swiftly behind him: at midnight, you'll find him
Where nightshade is blooming — that greedy old sinner
The Ghoul is consuming *a seven-corpse dinner.*

Originally published in *Weird Tales*, Summer 1988.

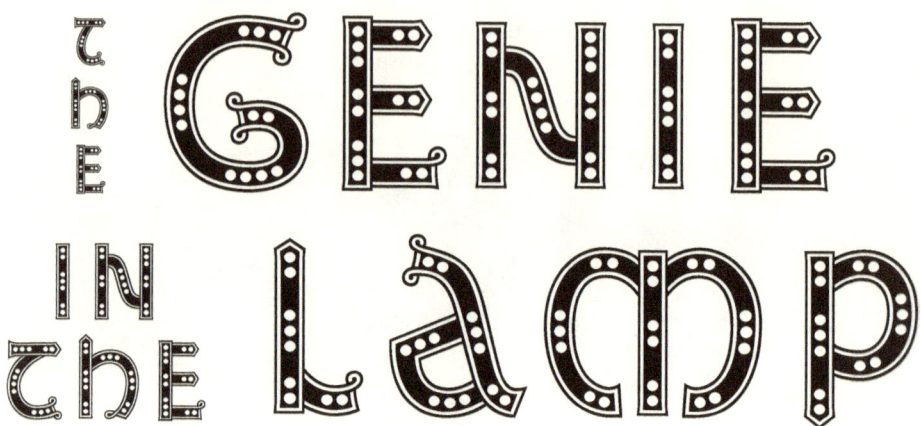

The GENIE in the LAMP

Secure and snug and cozy is the lamp in which I dwell,
The lamp in which I fashion mystic lore and magic spell,
And dream of eldritch fantasies no mortal mind can tell.
No mortal eyes can penetrate the lair in which I camp,
But just when I get settled down
. . . some moron rubs the lamp!
And everyone who rubs my lamp,
No matter what their name,
Makes a wish — and all those wishes
Sound unbearably the same:
For it's

"Gimme money! Gimme pearls! Gimme sixty naked girls!
Gimme diamonds! Gimme dough! Gimme Marilyn Monroe!
Gimme a brand-new Cadillac! Gimme, gimme! Yak, yak, yak!"
I grant their wishes and do as they bid,
Get back in my lamp, and close the lid.
Now then, where was I? Ah, yes . . .

Serene and calm and tranquil is this lamp, my habitat.
I dine on figs and honey from the cliffs of Ararat
And make sure all the harem girls can see my welcome mat.
Beneath Egyptian pyramids I court a sultry vamp,
And just when things start looking good
. . . some moron rubs the lamp!
And it's

Originally published in *Isaac Asimov's Science Fiction Magazine*, August 1981.

"Gimme silver! Gimme jewels! Turn my in-laws into mules!
Gimme a million bucks or so! Gimme a ham on rye to go!
Make me Sultan! Make me Shah! Gimme, gimme! Blah, blah, blah!"
The Brotherhood of Genies (Local Seven Thirty-Two)
Says I have to grant the wishes all these jerks would have me do.
So I bring them oils and spices and I bring them golden fleece,
But one rub on my lamp and
All hopes have been dampened
That they'll ever leave me in peace.
They rub my lamp and wish for half the riches in creation;
(Well, I'd sure hate to sadden some budding Aladdin
But frankly, I need a vacation.)

I'm not granting any more wishes.
Don't rub on my lamp; I'm not in.
So if any of you have one wish (or a few)
That you wish would come true, then the thing you should do
Is forget about Genies with lamps that you rub,
And pick up your wishes, and go to the pub,
And make friends with a bottle of *Djinn*.

CONFESSION TIME: In July 2000, while I was designing page layouts for
this book, the U.S. Congress held hearings on the legality of a website
which enabled the copying of MP3 music recordings free of charge,
with no payment accruing to the artists who created that music.
A very well-paid drum-banger for a well-known rock band testified
before Congress, objecting to the website's unauthorised use of his songs.
My reaction to his testimony was roughly like this: *'Poor crybaby.*
Instead of making $100 million a year, he has to scrape along on a
mere $90 million. I wish that anything at all *which I created was*
popular enough that someone would want to steal it.'

Literally *the very next day* after I made this moral observation,
I discovered that some jumped-up little bastard in Chandler, Arizona
(I shan't mention his name) had got hold of my poem *'The Genie in the
Lamp'*. He made a few 'improvements' in my text, and he posted it on his
website without my permission. His web page identified me as the author
of this 'improved' version of my poem, but he did not acknowledge my
copyright, nor did he offer me any payment. As you may guess, I was not
best pleased by his unauthorised use of my poetry, and I took legal action
. . . even though, only one day earlier on, I had condoned the theft of a
rock drummer's music.

So, whenever I think of *'The Genie in the Lamp'*, I can't help but
remember that I'm capable of hypocrisy. I'll start worrying about this
when poets are as rich as rock musicians.

The
Vanishing Man

I'll tell you the tale (just as quick as I can)
Of the day I discovered the Vanishing Man.
In a field north of Nashville, I happened to meet
A man who was real, but he seemed incomplete.
Then I noticed the problem: *he didn't have feet!*
His legs finished off where his ankles began.

"I'm stuck! Help me out!" said the man with a shout,
And his legs with no feet dangled over the ground.
"I'm stuck in some hole I can't see or control . . ."
Then his knees slowly vanished, not making a sound.

I ran to him then with all possible haste,
And I got a firm grip on the man by his waist.
Then I pulled and I tugged just as hard as I could.
I groaned and I strained, but it wasn't much good;
He was stuck, like a tree, rooted right where he stood.
And then both his legs were quite simply *erased.*

He yelled *"It's no use! I can't seem to get loose!"*
And he floated, a man with no legs, in midair.
"Let go! Leave me be! Or you'll vanish like me!"
Then I looked for his hips, but *they just weren't there.*

I ran to fetch rope, for I thought a rope might
Save the Vanishing Man (though his chances were slight).
By the time I returned, it was worse than I'd feared:
His stomach and chest, they had both disappeared . . .
And he'd vanished right up to the tip of his beard!
Then his head, while I watched, began fading from sight.

He started to cry: *"What is happening? Why?"*
But the rest of his voice faded, faint and unknown.
The bits of his face slowly vanished from space
And I found myself standing there, cold and alone.

But where did he go? Well, I cannot ignore
One historical fact: *Men have vanished before.*
And at night, in my nightmares, I see them inside
A specimen jar, or a microscope slide,
And I wonder: *Is there any place I can hide*
If whatever collected them comes back for more?

> As I mentioned in the foreword to this volume,
> *'The Vanishing Man'* was inspired by *'Jim Jay'*, a
> science-fiction poem by Walter de la Mare. In order
> to avoid copying Mr de la Mare's creation too closely,
> I was careful to use a completely original rhyme
> scheme and metre for my own version.
>
> If you're not familiar with the fantasy verses
> of Walter de la Mare, you've missed something
> wondrous indeed. I strongly suggest that you seek
> out a collection of his poems . . . and *enjoy.*

Originally published in *Amazing Stories*, May 1984.

THE OGRE

Early one morning, without any warning,
While both of his parents lay dreaming,
Young Johnny fell out
Of his bed with a shout
And he ran down the corridor, screaming.

"An Ogre is under my bed!" Johnny cried,
When his parents both asked what was wrong.
"An Ogre with long hairy fingers *this* wide,
And his sharp pointy teeth are *this* long!
His skin is all green, and he looks really mean,
And he grinned and he laughed
And made all kinds of noise
And he said: *'I'm an Ogre! I KILL LITTLE BOYS!'*
He's under my bed!
Take a look!" Johnny said,
And his five-year-old face had turned white.
"He said: *'I'll go away, little boy, for today,*
BUT I'LL COME BACK AND KILL YOU TONIGHT!' "

"What a nightmare you had,"
Said his parents, and smiled.
"What a dreamer, that lad. What a boy! What a child!"
They would not even *look* underneath Johnny's bed.
For the Ogre was only a nightmare, they said.

56

But his grandmother came and she took Johnny's hand,
And she spoke in a way little boys understand:
"There will always be Ogres to scare you," she said,
"And monsters will always be under your bed.
You can't run away from the shadows of fear.
But the way to erase them
Is: stand up and face them
And fight them and chase them, and they'll disappear . . ."

So Johnny went back to his bedroom that night
And he lay in the stillness, alone with his fright,
And he tried very hard not to cry.
And the Ogre came at him from under the bed
And its long yellow fingers encircled his head
And the Ogre said: ***"Johnny! GET READY TO DIE!"***

*   *   *

Next morning the house was as still as a tomb;
No sound emanated from young Johnny's room.
But from under the door, all along the bare floor,
Trickled something unpleasant and red.
And his parents, not knowing what they should expect,
Broke open his door and they found the place wrecked.
But they pulled Johnny free from beneath the debris,
And he managed to stand, and he pointed his hand
At a thing in the corner that quivered and bled,
And the boy told his mother: *"The Ogre is dead."*

Originally published in *Amazing Stories*, March 1985.

The Beast in the Loch

Softly and silently, secret and swift.
Deep in the loch . . . down to the sea . . .
Down where the dark dreams of centuries drift,
I am the child of the sea.
Long before Caesar came marching through Gaul,
Long before Hadrian built his great wall,
I was here waiting and witnessed them all:
I am the serpent who swims to the sea . . .

Swiftly and secretly, safe and secure.
Deep in the loch . . . mystical loch . . .
Down where the water is crystal and pure,
I am the child of the sea.
Here Saint Columba knelt down and he prayed.
Here knights of Cromwell prepared for the raid.
I came before them, and here I have stayed:
I am the serpent who swims to the sea . . .

Scientists come, with a diving machine.
Let them come! Let them camp on the banks of my shore!
Curious onlookers, eager and keen:
Let them come, as their ancestors came here before!
Hydrophone crews in a steel submarine . . .
Sonar and radar for *Time* magazine . . .
Let them come if they can! Let them seek the unseen!
While deep in the loch I lie safe and serene,
For I am the daughter of legend and water.
    I am the child . . . ancient and wild . . .
        I am the child of the sea.

Softly and silently, secret and swift.
Deep in the loch . . . ancient grey loch . . .
Life everlasting: a curse, or a gift?
I am as old as the sea.
Timeless, I drift while the centuries creep.
Men live and die, laugh and cry, love and weep,
Never suspecting the secrets I keep:
I am the serpent, and cry in my sleep . . .

Originally published in *Isaac Asimov's Science Fiction Magazine*, May 1981.

Parodies, Limericks, Fragments & Filks

Among the strange people you'll meet at a typical science-fiction convention are the *filk singers*: musical groups (often with excellent voices) who provide *a capella** performances of 'filk songs'. There's no official definition of this term; filk songs (or 'filks') are usually musical mongrels: new parody lyrics grafted onto a well-known tune. The songs performed by Allan Sherman in the 1960s were proto-filks, although the term didn't originate until after his death. But many filkers are talented composers, and some of the best filk songs feature original melodies. Filking is like *karaoke*: anyone can join in, and enthusiasm is more filkworthy than talent. To ensure that everyone knows the tune (and to avoid copyright problems), filk lyrics are usually set to traditional folk melodies, sea chanteys, or old-time show tunes that are now in the public domain.

Most filk songs are parodies, and some (not all) of them can get fairly raunchy. Hence the origin of the term: if you add a filthy lyric to a folk song, you've got a filthy folk song . . . or a *filk song* for short.

Here are some verses and lyrics that don't fit the theme of my **Improbable Bestiary**. I've included two of my filks — *"Doin' the Prime Directive"* and *"Donovan's Mikado"* — which I've sung at filkfests and informal eisteddfods† in Britain, America and Australia. You are welcome to perform these songs in any *amateur* venue of your choosing. (If anyone charges money, I'll be expecting a share.)

If you've enjoyed this collection of verses, then my Bestiary has served its purpose. Will there be a sequel? Yes, if I can corral enough crypto-critters to fill a second volume. But, alas, even poets must eat . . . and the cruel economics of publishing guarantee that even a very good book of poems will make much less money than a very bad novel.‡ If I'm not writing as much poetry as I used to, it's because — like Willie Sutton, the patron saint of publishers — I must go where the money is.

Still, for now, here are two of my filks . . .

☞

---

* This is a fancy phrase which means 'We're too cheap to buy musical instruments, and we can't play them anyway.'

† This is a typographical error.

‡ And a bloody-awful screenplay will make the most money of all.

Doin' the Prime Directive

In 1993, I went to Hollywood to pitch script ideas to the producers of ***Star Trek: The Next Generation***. I knew that several of this show's cast members were talented singers and dancers, who were frustrated by the fact that ***Star Trek***'s non-musical storylines did not give them many opportunities to showcase their musical talents.

Hence my brilliant idea. I pitched to the producers a spec script titled *That's My Q*, in which the fiendish alien named Q kidnaps the crew of the *Enterprise* and forces them to star in an intergalactic musical revue. A plotline of this sort requires bouncy melodies and scintillating lyrics, so I wrote a dozen slam-bang up-tempo numbers for the *Enterprise* officers to perform. I was careful to give each of the main cast members a solo number with a socko finish. Since Q is an omniscient entity who can easily contravene the laws of nature, I gave him a fast patter song with tongue-twisting lyrics.

In the event, the ***Star Trek*** producers listened to all my material, promised to get back to me . . . and never did so. The musical episode of ***Star Trek*** has never seen the light of day. Until now.

I offer here a tantalising sample from the score of my unproduced masterpiece: the music and words for a song to be performed by Jean-Luc Picard, the captain of the starship *Enterprise*. (One line is sung by Worf, the Klingon *basso profundo*. The notes with no words underneath them are dance music.) If any producers out there are seeking a talented composer/lyricist to write the score for their next musical, I hope that they'll contact me.

PICARD: We have a creed; let's make it clear: don't in - ter - cede, don't in - ter - fere. That's what we call do - in' the Prime Di - rec - tive! We are -n't thieves,

we are -n't spies; Star-fleet be - lieves it would be wise

if we were all do - in' the Prime Di - rec - tive!

As we ex-plore each new di - men - sion,

we would-n't dream of in - ter-

- ven - tion! WORF: It's nev-er our in - ten - tion!

PICARD: And if you choose to bring a gun, make sure you use

pha - sers on "stun"! Then, if you meet a - li - en slime,

beat a re-treat back-wards through Time! Here in the Fleet,

we do the Prime Di - rec - tive! (spoken:) *Make it so!*

One evening in 1985, I attended an amateur performance of Gilbert & Sullivan's **The Mikado**, then returned home in time for a late-night screening of the classic horror movie **Donovan's Brain** (starring the young Nancy Reagan). This ditty is the unholy result. It may be sung to the tune of *'Tit-Willow'*. (Is a tit willow any relation to a pussy willow? I'm just wondering.)

In order for the choruses to rhyme, you should pronounce the word 'data' with the Victorian pronunciation 'DAT-tuh'. My apologies to Mister Data of the starship *Enterprise*, who favours a different pronunciation.

DONOVAN'S MIKADO;
or, *I've Got a Little Lust*

In a jar in the lab I discovered a brain
That said *"Data, more data, more data."*
How it spoke is a thing which I cannot explain;
It said *"Data, more data, more data."*
So I said to it: "Brain, tell me why do you stew
In a pickle-jar full of formaldehyde goo?"
But the brain merely answered, as brains often do:
"Give me data, more data, more data."

Then I said: "Tell me, brain, did your body decay?
Were your organs removed like errata?
Did some scientist throw your whole body away,
And regard it *persona non grata?*
Can you feel much?" I asked. "Are you conscious of pain?"
But there came no reply from that pickle-jar brain;
All it did was continue its endless refrain:
"Give me data, more data, more data.

"I shall conquer the world," said the brain. *"I shall rule
While I float in this jar of phlegmata."*
Then the brain bobbed about in its chemical pool
While it chortled a gleeful cantata.
"I'll enslave all mankind," said that sinister brain,
*"And the whole planet Earth will become my domain,
But before I take over, I'll have to obtain
Much more data, more data, more data."*

"Too bad," I remarked, "but your plan of attack
Comes with certain small flaws and stigmata."
Then I carried the brain to a cesspool out back
That descends through the bedrock and strata.
"Happy landings!" I said, and I dropped it inside.
"Let me out!" shrieked the brain. As it fell, I replied:
"Out of *where?* When and how? Please, you'll have to provide
Much more data, more data, more data!"

Originally published in *Amazing Stories*, July 1986.

A book tour once brought me to Baltimore, where a literary critic told me that my stories and verses were comparable to the works of Edgar Allan Poe . . . at least, I *think* that's what he meant. His exact words to me were: 'Man, you are the *Poe*-est writer!'

Edgar Allan Poe, who was a raven maniac, never explained why the raven in his poem was so talkative. I think the raven spoke because it had sufficient caws. Which brings me to . . .

The Long-Lost First Draft of 'The Raven'

Once upon a midnight dreary,
While I pondered, bleak and bleary,
Contemplating *hara-kiri* —
Seeking Death's eternal shore —
All at once, my grim surrounding
Rang with echoes most astounding:
Sounding just like someone pounding,
Hounding me outside my door.
(Bill collectors. Nothing more.)

Then there came a crash of thunder
As my door-frame smashed asunder
And I gaped in helpless wonder
As a shape began to loom;
Through the entrance to my study
Came somebody damp and muddy
Dripping cruddy window-putty
All across the ruddy room.
(Traveling salesman, I assume.)

Then I felt my senses cave in
When I saw this was a *Raven*
That had entered, seeking haven
From the storm beyond my door.
Searching out a place for perching,
Thus it entered, wildly lurching,
Both its filthy feet besmirching
Mud across my chamber floor.
(Which I'd swept the day before.)

Thus provok'd, I fell to raging,
And I contemplated waging
Wrath and ire beyond assuaging
On this bird. (Revenge is sweet.)
"Fiend!" I shrieked, in rage aortal.
"Raven, are ye ghoul or mortal?
Look: you've muddied up my portal;
Don't you ever *wipe your feet?*
Answer, or you'll fill a coffin!"

Quoth the Raven: *"Not too often."*

Originally published in *Amazing Stories*, January 1986, with a slightly different title: "The Long-Lost First Draft of Edgar Allan Poe's 'The Raven'".

4 *from* **Literary Review**

In January 2001, whilst I was preparing the galley proofs for this collection of my poems, word reached me of the sudden death of Auberon Waugh. All poets and poetry-lovers should take notice. Apart from being the eldest son of the author of **Brideshead Revisited**, Auberon Waugh (known to his friends as 'Bron') was also a respected journalist, a prolific diarist, a literary critic, an authority on wine, and — most importantly — the editor of *Literary Review*.

We first crossed paths in 1993, when — after a visit to the U.S.A. — Mr Waugh wrote an essay for the English magazine *The Spectator* in which he complained that Americans have names which conceal their gender. He claimed that he could never tell, from the name alone, whether any specific American is either male or female.

I promptly fired off a letter to *The Spectator*, in which I asked: 'Is this Mr Waugh's own observation, or did he get it from the novels written by his mother Evelyn?' To his credit, Auberon Waugh saw the point of my joke,* and he was so amused by it that he invited me to a literary function at his home in Somerset. I never quite managed to earn a place within his innermost circle (there was much competition for that honour), but we did become colleagues, and friends.

In my never-ending battle to rescue poetry from the pretentious blank-versers and drivel-smiths who detest rhyme and metre, I often feel like a lone voice in the wilderness. Yet Bron Waugh achieved far more than I can ever hope to accomplish for the sacred cause of *real* poetry, the sort that rhymes and makes sense. From his high pulpit as editor of *Literary Review*, he conducted a relentless campaign for poetry that *follows the rules*.

As I write these words — less than a fortnight after Bron's death — I don't know yet if his editorial successors at *Literary Review* will

---

* I meant, of course, that any man whose *father* was named Evelyn has no reason to criticise other people with hermaphroditic monickers. My witticism was made even sharper by the fact that Evelyn Waugh's first wife was *also* named Evelyn, thus adding to the gender confusion and undercutting Auberon's argument even further. The *female* Evelyn Waugh was not Auberon's mother, although she might arguably be deemed his stepmother . . . and I feel that any man whose father and stepmother were *both* named Evelyn has no business making fun of Americans. If any literary historians (or anyone else with too much free time) should like to read the full text of my letter to *The Spectator*, it was published in their 13 March 1993 number.

continue his crusade. Under Bron Waugh's stewardship, every issue of *Literary Review* from 1987 onwards featured a poetry contest, in which he challenged all comers to write a poem that rhymed, scanned, and intelligibly addressed the contest's theme (which was different each month). Each month's entries were judged by a jury of poetry lovers, headed by Auberon Waugh; the best poems in each batch won cash prizes — the upper-level prizes being very nice amounts of moolah indeed — and all of the winning entries were published in *Literary Review* and in annual book-length compilations. I hope that this tradition will continue in the post-Waugh *Literary Review*. I submitted quite a few of my own poems to his monthly contests: not only for the chance of winning more lolly than I was ever likely to be paid for my poetic efforts elsewhere, but also because I enjoyed the challenge of writing poetry to a theme which someone else had chosen for me.

Although I have never yet copped the grand prize in *Literary Review*'s monthly poetry contest, here are four of my entries which attained the lower rungs of Auberon Waugh's esteem, and all of which were first published in *Literary Review*. In the September 1997 issue, the contest's theme was 'Water' . . . so I perversely wrote a poem that never includes the word 'water' at all:

AQUA VIVA

I am the endless tides of time,
I flowed through pre-Silurian slime,
Through dust, through rust, through grit, through grime.
Flow on, flow on forever.

I am the Bible's ancient Flood,
I am the rains, the sleet, the mud.
Within your veins, I'm in your blood.
Flow on, flow on forever.

I slaked the thirst of emperors and quenched the sweat of slaves.
Yet man's eternal tyranny has never tamed my waves.
I cushion babes within the womb, and seep through mouldy graves.
Flow Rubicon, flow Amazon, flow on and on and free.

I am the storm, the tempest's brew,
The mists of dawn, the evening dew.
I'm sixty-five per cent of *you*.
I am the sea,
Eternally . . .
Flow on, flow on forever.

For the February 1997 *Literary Review*, the theme was 'Stalking'
... and I wrote accordingly. For the benefit of American readers,
I should explain two references in this poem: Knickerbox is a
British-based chain of upscale lingerie shops, and John Menzies
is a chain of news agents.

I SAW YOU

I saw you in Knickerbox, buying your tights,
And I watched you outside the John Menzies.
I've seen you go dancing on Saturday nights,
And you dance in my dreams and my frenzies.
I practise my lurk in the place where you work,
So I know when and where I can find you
And I know the whole route of your daily commute;
On the bus, I was sitting behind you.
You probably claim that you don't know my name,
And I've seen you pretend to ignore me
But I know for a fact that it's all just an act
To conceal that you really adore me.
You prove — when you talk, when you move, when you walk —
That you're thinking about me, you can't live without me.
And when you're alone, you can bet that I'll phone you
And whisper the places I've seen you and known you.
I'll haunt you, and taunt you, and daunt you: *I own you.*

Auberon Waugh had appreciated my verses even before we met,
because I was already a loyal reader of *Literary Review* and a winner
(strictly lower-echelon) in his monthly poetry competitions. For the
theme of the December 1992 contest, poets were challenged to offer
'An Author's Lament' . . . and we were told to take a masochistic
tone in our entries. I hope that no armchair psychiatrists will draw
conclusions about me from the self-pitying flavour of the following:

IMMORTALITY

Oh, pulp my gonads and my guts together,
And slice them into crisp octavo pages.
Transform my flesh to sweet Morocco leather
In which to bind my prose for future ages.
    Scourge me or purge me or brutally bleed me;
    After I'm dead, only promise you'll READ ME!

Come vent my spleen, eviscerate my vitals —
My blood shall be the ink my printers use —
Upon my cranium, engrave the titles
Of all my books, as well as my reviews.
   Publishers' cheques were too meagre to feed me;
   After I'm dead, only promise you'll READ ME!

My flesh and form inevitably perish —
My heart runs out of ink, and dries to crust —
Yet one thing I've produced that you must cherish
When all my self has mouldered into dust.
   Death from starvation has finally freed me,
   Still I can speak to the souls who succeed me:
   Prove you will need me,
     and heed me,
      and READ ME!

For the March 1992 issue, contestants were required to submit
a poem which paid tribute to any British literary figure of their choice.
Here's my contribution, which is now (so he tells me, at least) one of
science-fiction author Charles Sheffield's favourite verses. Although
I won a prize for this, there are no prizes for guessing which literary
figure (not actually British-born) I chose to honour:

RUDDY

I walks into a college quad, in 'opes of some respect.
A student sneers and says I hain't Politically Correct.
The arty-tarty critics deconstruct me, bit by bit,
So I chucks that bloomin' Bloomsb'ry mob and answers back, to wit:
"Oh, it's Ruddy this and Bloody that, and 'Jingo fascist brute!'
But it's 'Bless you, Mister Kipling' when the guns begin to shoot.
I wrote the sort of verse what Oxford toffee-noses shun,
But it's 'Thank you, Mister Kipling' when a battle's to be won!"

All I arsk in terms of honour is a fragment of respect,
(Though I ain't no bleedin' Kafka, nor leastways no Bertholt Brecht.)
I don't want no bloomin' glory; that's for heroes, I'll be bound.
(Like my son, who fought for England, and who died on foreign ground.)
Honour? Glory? Did I earn 'em? Maybe that's the reason why
I was placed in Poets' Corner. (Charlie Dickens sleeps nearby.)
When it comes to barrack-ballads, I was Britain's bloomin' bard;
I'm the man whose name was Kipling . . . and I tried so *Ruddy 'ard!*

And may I take this opportunity to say: **Thank you, Bron Waugh**.

All Hail the Lowly Limerick!

The limerick, widely assumed to be a Victorian invention, is really far older . . . dating back to Shakespeare's time, if not beyond it. In **Othello**, Act 2, scene 3, lines 69–73, the evil ensign Iago chants a drinking-song which conforms almost precisely to the structure of a limerick. I shan't render Iago's limerick here for you, because I want you to look it up. (Everyone should read some Shakespeare every day.)

You may have wondered if any link exists between *limericks* and the county, city or borough of Limerick in Ireland. The answer to this is: none at all.

Often, when a poet invents a new verse-form (or takes an existing verse-form and develops it further), this sort of verse will acquire the name of its patron poet. For example, a type of ode developed by the Greek poet Pindar is now called a *pindaric*. The poetess Sappho of Lesbos — yes, she was a Lesbian — favoured a form of stanza verse that is now known as a *sapphic*.

The first poet to make conspicuous use of the limerick form was, of course, Edward Lear (1812 – 1888). There was no name for such poems at the time, so he called them *nonsense verses*. Lear created so many limericks, of such delightful content, that his readers assumed he had *invented* this particular form of verse. (A claim which Lear himself never made.) Nonsense verses employing Lear's AABBA structure became known as *Learic rhymes*.

But the word *'Learic'* sounds too much like *'lyric'*, a word which describes any short poem that can be sung. All Learics are lyrics but not all lyrics are Learics. Some other name was needed for these cunning little verses. Eventually, someone's tongue stumbled over the phrase 'Learic rhymes', and — in an act of metathesis[1] — *Learic rhymes* became *Leamric ryes*. The road from 'Leamric' to 'Limerick' was short, and the journey a happy one. Along the road to Limerick we meet such delightful people as the young man from Devizes (whose *things* were of two different sizes), the man from Australia

---

[1] *Metathesis* is a fancy name for that slip of the tongue when a piece of one word is accidentally transferred to another word, or two pieces are transposed. If you want some streaky bacon, but you accidentally ask for *'strakey beacon'*, that's a metathesis. If you do it deliberately, in an attempt to be funny, it's a spoonerism. In the 1930s, an American radio comedian named Colonel Stoopnagle had a comedy routine based almost entirely on spoonerisms. It wobbably pruzzn't foo tunny.

(whose life was a definite failure)[2], and my own favourite: the girl from Nantucket.

Here are four of my own limericks:

That Settles That

Gentle Reader, you may wonder: *Why Isn't "S.F." the same as "Sci-Fi"?* Well, you see, there's a fine line Between Robert Heinlein And *Son of the Two-Headed Fly.*

In this next *opus horribilis*, the word at the end of the first line is pronounced 'Oh-fee-YOO-kuss'.[3]

Coming Soon to a Planet Near You

The creatures from far Ophiuchus Have gleefully threatened to nuke us. Well, if they *do* bomb us, I hope that they promise To sell the film rights to George Lucas.

In 1983, I made a 'break a leg' phone call from my summer home at Bryn Awel, Pentraeth, to novelist John Brunner in Borgomanero, Italy, where he was to speak at a science-fiction convention. John loved Italy — far more than his native England — and he visited that country as often as possible. During our phone chat, John and I exchanged a few pungent puns and livid limericks, and then he told me that he planned to return to Italy for his 50th birthday in September 1984. With his characteristic generosity, John told me that — if I could arrange my own transport — I was welcome to attend his birthday celebration in Italy, which promised to be an event of riotous debauchery and several days' duration.

'That Settles That' was first published in *Isaac Asimov's Science Fiction Magazine*, July 1980.

'Coming Soon to a Planet Near You' was first published — with an incorrect title — in *Isaac Asimov's Science Fiction Magazine*, July 1981.

---

[2] I've always assumed that this limerick was written about *me*. And I can't think why.

[3] *Ophiuchus* is a constellation located spang-dab in the middle of the zodiac . . . and astrologers wish that it would go away, or at least move elsewhere in the sky. Astrologers (also known as 'crooks') have neatly divided the zodiac into twelve equal slices, with a constellation ruling each. Since there are twelve months in the year and twelve signs in the zodiac, all the people who are born within the same 30-day interval are ruled (it says here) by the same sign of the zodiac. Unfortunately for astrologers (but fortunately for common sense), the region of the night sky which is known as the zodiac actually contains *thirteen* constellations, the thirteenth being Ophiuchus. Whenever anybody asks me 'What's your sign?' I invariably reply 'Ophiuchus'. If anyone fails to take the hint, and asks me 'No, no: what sign were you *born* under?' I answer 'Low Headroom'.

Of course, it would never do if I arrived empty-handed, so for my trip to John's festivities in 1984 I brought along a limerick, especially written for the occasion . . . and smuggled into Italy under the noses of the border guards. John was interested in Roman history, and so — as a more tangible memento of his fiftieth birthday — I also gave him a copy of his age in Roman numerals, in the form of a learner plate.[4]

Like many other fiftyish men, John worried about his dwindling virility. I addressed this concern in my limerick, with appropriate Roman numerals. 'Goolies' is a British slang word for a certain portion of the male anatomy:

Happy Birthday, John Brunner
As for birthdays, it pains me to tell,
At age 40, a man can XL.
But if, at age 50,
His goolies should drift, he
Can still lift his glass. What the L.

After hearing John Brunner recite his limerick about the farmer from Kirkcudbright (which has been published elsewhere), I fired this rejoinder across John's gunwales. You'll have to figure out the pronunciations for yourself, but that's part of the fun. This limerick suffered in obscurity for more than ten years (and rightly so) without a title, but I gave it a title in 1994 after *l'affaire* Lorena Bobbitt:[5]

The Ballad of Ewan Owain ap Bwbytt
A Welshman from old Aberystwyth
Had a mistress he'd frequently trystwyth.
Till his mortified wife
Took a large carving-knife
And she sliced off the bit that he pystwyth.

And that's quite enough limericks . . .

---

[4] This was, of course, just a capital L. In Britain, student motorists must engage in public humiliation (another great British tradition) by displaying prominently, on their vehicles, stark proof of their novitiate status in the form of a large scarlet letter 'L' . . . which (depending on the driver) stands either for Learner or for *Look Out!*

[5] This limerick has never been published before, and a damned good thing it hasn't been. 'Ewan Owain ap Bwbytt' is my attempt at a Welsh approximation of the name 'John Wayne Bobbitt'. Mr J W Bobbitt, as you may recall, was the gentleman who had regular access to his wife's sexual favours until she decided to cut him off. Nasty business, that was.

Dear Doctor Asimov. . .

In the late 1970s, while living in Britain, I encountered an excellent American periodical called *Isaac Asimov's Science Fiction Magazine*. The famous Doctor Asimov was too busy to edit this magazine himself, but he did have considerable input as a contributor, and he also served as advisor to the editor George Scithers. I straight away submitted several of my best science-fiction manuscripts to Mr Scithers, and he straight away sent them right back to me with lovely little rejection slips.

Among his many other merits, Dr Asimov was always an advocate of poetry that rhymes and follows a coherent metre. In 1979, he invited his magazine's readers to participate in an *acrostic sonnet* contest. A sonnet, of course, is a 14-line poem which conforms to certain structural rules. An *acrostic* sonnet is even trickier: the fourteen letters at the front of the poem — the first letter of each line — must spell out, in order, a 14-letter message. In Asimov's contest, every sonnet had to rhyme, make sense and *also* spell out an acrostic message. And since the winning sonnet would be published in *Isaac Asimov's Science Fiction Magazine*, the poem (and its hidden message) had to be *about* some aspect of science fiction.

I am always eager to accept a challenge (providing it doesn't involve any hard work), so I dashed off not one but *four* different acrostic sonnets, each employing a different rhyme scheme. Months later, I was gobsmacked to receive the news that one of my four entries had been chosen by Dr Asimov as the winner of his contest, and he promptly published it in the February 1980 issue of his magazine. Here is my winning sonnet, and I'm sure that you will have no difficulty discovering its hidden message:

Gee whiz, I hope he buys this thing I wrote!

(**E**xactly why he *should*, I couldn't say.)

Oh, gosh! I wonder just how much he'll *pay?*

(**R**emind me to attach a little note.)

Gee whillikers, it really gets my goat!

Eight days I've waited! What's the big delay?

Supposing he rejects it right away?

(**C**ome back next week and watch me slit my throat.)

If he just *likes* it, I'll be satisfied.

Too bad I don't know how he works or thinks.

Hey! He might even *buy* it! Well, he *might!*

Eureka! Here's his letter! What's inside?

"**R**egarding your submission, bub: it STINKS!

Say, pal, whoever told you you could write?"

But there could only be *one* winning entry in Doctor Asimov's contest, and I had submitted *four* acrostic sonnets . . . which gave me a mathematical certainty that at least *three* of my entries would be losers. Proud as I am of my victorious sonnet, I believe that another one of my efforts from the same four-sonnet batch is much better than the one which Doctor Asimov chose. But judge for yourself. Published here, for the first time anywhere — please try to contain your excitement — is my acrostic sonnet which (sez me) *should* have won the contest:

Sit back, and feel your mind unloose its ties,

Cast off its moorings, soar off wild and free

Into an alternate reality;

Escape from earthbound ways to star-filled skies.

Now READ! Aye, read in wonder and surprise . . .

Consider: can such marvels truly *be?*

Excitement! For at last your mind can see

Far more than you'd perceive with mundane eyes.

Imagine! You're in some far-distant realm . . .

Create! An odyssey through Space and Time . . .

Take off! A ship to Mars; *you're* at the helm . . .

Invent! A bug-eyed monster, oozing slime.

On every page, the senses overwhelm;

Now, come: experience a world sublime . . .

In the summer of 1980, at the World Science Fiction Convention in Boston, Massachusetts, I had the honour of *meeting* Isaac Asimov, and the privilege — from then until his death — of remaining his friend. Of course, we sometimes pranked each other. In the March 1981 issue of his magazine, Isaac claimed (I quote from memory) that poetry is inferior to fiction, since poetry (he alleged) is less coherent than prose. This got my dander up (my dander gets up easily), because I know that poetry — *good* poetry — is able to convey just as much content and meaning as any other narrative form. To prove my point, I fired off a massive missive to the editorial offices of *Asimov's Science Fiction Magazine.* But (once again) judge for yourself; here is my letter, which was published as the lead-off correspondence in the August 1981 number of that periodical:

Dear Doctor Asimov:

I enjoy your monthly column, sir, but wish to disagree with your piece in March's issue and your views on poetry. Yes, it's true that there are poets who don't make a lot of sense, but so many *fiction* writers perpetrate the same offence. I have heard some strange opinions, and the strangest ones are those which purport to prove that poetry's inferior to prose. I agree that writing fiction is a complicated skill, but to write successful poetry is even harder still! Now a fiction work is boring, weak, and dull unless it's got things like narrative and character and (most of all) a plot; fiction writers must know grammar, punctuation, form, and tense . . . and the actions of the characters should make dramatic sense. And you *must* be entertaining, or your tale's not worth a dime. But a poet must do all of the above . . . AND ALSO *RHYME!* There are certain forms of poetry — like tanka and haiku — which describe a static scene and then that's all they ever do. But the modern sort of poet writing *modern* verses knows that the work must tell a story and have action (just like prose) and it's got to have a plot that entertains you every time. What I mean is, it's a *story* . . . but the story has to *RHYME!*

Well, I'd rather not pack entire pages this way.

Fondly,

— *F. Gwynplaine MacIntyre*

London, U.K.

I was later informed, by an editorial minion who was present when my letter arrived in the postbag, that every member of the office staff burst into laughter while reading it . . . everyone, that is, *except* Doctor Asimov, who *didn't notice* (so I'm told) that I had demonstrated my point by writing my letter entirely in rhymed metric verse, including the signature. Reportedly, when someone finally let Isaac in on the joke, he read my letter again, roared with laughter, and insisted that it be published in the letters column.

I have difficulty believing that Isaac failed to notice, the first time round, that my letter was written in rhyme. Among his many talents, Isaac Asimov was a versifier and lyricist in his own right. On several occasions during our friendship, he and I made informal attempts to collaborate on the libretto of a science-fiction operetta titled **Starship Pinafore**, intending to add our own original lyrics to Gilbert's plotline and Sullivan's music. I very much regret that this project never saw the light of day.

But I have continued to insist that rhymed verse, when properly done, is a suitable vehicle for *telling a story* which has a beginning, a middle and a conclusion: just like any other narrative art form. Which brings me (and you, on the next page) to the subject of *'OOPS!'* . . .

OOPS!

'*OOPS!*' is one of my pushmi-pullyu attempts to write something which is poetry and prose <u>both at once</u>. '*OOPS!*' tells a linear story (like prose) but it's written in metric verse (like poetry). Just to be extra-specially fiendish, I deliberately had the whole thing typeset as running text, like a conventional story — rather than breaking it line-for-line, like verse — so that readers *might not notice* straight off that they were reading poetry.

<u>Some</u> readers noticed, though, because '*OOPS!*' was nominated for the 1991 Rhysling Award as best science-fiction poem of the year. 'Nominated', of course, is a fancy way of saying 'didn't win'. One of these days, I really must slip a quick fiver to the Rhysling judges.

Anyway, here's '*OOPS!*':

> The famous Professor Fallopius Fitch discovered a wonderful Theory which explained in precise mathematical terms the Meaning of Life and the purpose of germs. It also explained, in a few simple words, the light of the stars and the language of birds.
> "All shades of the spectrum, whatever their pitch, fit into my Theory!" cried Doctor Fitch.
> And that wasn't all: every fish in the sea fit right into his Theory, neat as could be. Doctor Fitch's great Theory clearly explained why the galaxies formed and the crescent moon waned. Quarks, quasars, and wormholes — gigantic or small — were explained by his Theory, once and for all.
> "Each quantum of Space-Time has got its own niche in my marvelous Theory!" cried Doctor Fitch.
> But then Doctor Fitch very suddenly saw that his wonderful Theory had a slight flaw: it explained the whole Cosmos with nary a hitch, *but his Theory couldn't explain Doctor Fitch!*
> "A mere detail," he said, "which is easily missed." Then he published his findings, and *ceased to exist.*

'*OOPS!*' first appeared in the March 1991 number of *Analog*, which was a personal triumph for me: the very first occasion when any of my writing was published in that distinguished magazine.

But as luck (or Sod's Law) would have it, a gremlin in the page make-up department omitted my name (and any mention of '*OOPS!*') from the table of contents for that issue of *Analog*. Worse luck, the people who compile bibliographies usually acquire their data by glancing at tables of contents — instead of reading the actual sources — so this error has compounded as the years roll on. All known databases indicate that no story named '*OOPS!*', no poem named '*OOPS!*', and no author named F. Gwynplaine MacIntyre exist anywhere within the pages of the March 1991 *Analog*.

When you consider that '*OOPS!*' is about a man who obliterated all proof of his own existence by the simple act of publishing his work, I can't help wondering if there's some sort of interdimensional conspiracy dedicated to the task of *de-happening* anyone who stumbles onto the secret of . . .

Erm, never mind. Forget I said anything.

STYX &
STONES

On the day that I died I performed suicide
With some cyanide pills and an axe.
As I chopped off my head, I just chuckled and said
"Now that *that's* come off, I can relax!"
But that Lucifer bloke, in a billow of smoke,
Took my soul down to Hell, locked in chains.
And, declining to burn it, he
Damned (through Eternity)
All my immortal remains . . .

Now I shovel the coal down in Satan's black hole.
(Hell has furnaces; I am the stoker.)
And (bemoaning my fate) I must sweep out the grate,
Then I polish the tongs and the poker.
But for ten seconds (once every twelve million years) . . .
"Down tools, lads!" an Imp shouts. I burst into cheers,
Rush upstairs to Heaven, take *one* desperate glimpse . . .
Then back down to Hell, where I'm seized by the Imps.
Twelve million more years 'til the next time! Ah, well . . .
Except for the tea-breaks, this job is pure Hell.

Originally published in *Worlds of Fantasy & Horror*, Winter 1997.

ARMAGEDDON OUT OF HERE

'Armageddon Out of Here' was originally published — with an incorrect title — in *Weird Tales*, Winter 1989.

Fasten your door-locks, for here come the Morlocks,
Two Werewolves, three Warlocks, nine Ghosts and a Goon.
At sea, on a freighter, Miss Evelyn Slater
Met something which ate her with knife, fork, and spoon.
Some friends of Godzilla ate downtown Manila;
A giant gorilla named Kong has appeared.
Amidst these confusions, here come the Venusians!
(Don't jump to conclusions, but something is *weird!*)

Oh, the death-toll increases (*Tra-la! Hi-de-ho!*)
While the Earth blows to pieces. (*Well, that's how things go!*)
Some creatures from Pluto have borrowed the Sun.
(They'll bring it right back, though, as soon as they're done.)
That monster behind you comes closer, and then you
Quite suddenly find you are next on his menu.
Some Zombies with knives are in search of spare parts.
(When Chthulhu arrives, then the fun *really* starts!)

Oh, Mankind meets its doom (*Tra-la-la! Whoop-tee-doo!*)
As the world goes Ka-Boom. (*And so what else is new?*)
At quarter past seven the Earth stopped its turning.
(But this can't be Heaven; I smell something burning.)
Some day you will die; your estate will be probate.
A week will go by, and your flesh will be crow-bait.
You cannot assume you'll be safe in your room
When the minions of Doom all come out of the tomb.

No matter where you place your head —
In upper berth, or lower bed —
No matter in which bunk you lie, the hideous Homunculi
Will tiptoe and creep through your dreams while you sleep
And they'll whisper these words in a nightmarish hush:
"You can't live forever! Die *now! BEAT THE RUSH!*"

In Praise of Prose

Those of you who are still awake may wonder why I published this book. The short and simple answer is *'To make money'*, but this answer is too short *and* too simple. The road to quick-'n'-easy wealth seldom passes through the realm of Poetry. No person with even a tenuous grasp on reality makes long-term plans to get rich as a *poet*. But, so long as wanna-be authors are permitted to palm off their rhymeless babblings as 'poetry', and so long as literary bigots continue to sneer at rhymed verse and to dismiss it as 'greeting-card stuff', then the entire poetic art form continues to be perceived as uncommercial, and *any* volume of verse will be a money-losing proposition.

To hell with starving in a garret, then, or whatever I'm supposed to do in order to maintain my credentials as a Sensitive Poet. Just like any seemingly normal person, I want to live comfortably. Many people who would turn up their noses at an anthology of poems will still shell out their shekels for a collection of short stories. So, just to juice up the sales of **MacIntyre's Improbable Bestiary**, and to add a few beans to my bank balance, I've included four of my science-fiction and fantasy stories . . . as a non-poetic bonus to escape poetic onus.

This is part of my fiendish plan to drive librarians and booksellers crazy. Since my anthology contains poetry *and* fiction, nobody will know whether to stock this book in the Poetry section or in the Prose department. In bookshops, does **MacIntyre's Improbable Bestiary** belong displayed among other works of Fiction in the front window, or should it end up in the usual place for books of Poetry: inside the trash compactor? Perhaps the best course of action would be to tear this book in half, and fling the pages in all directions at once.

On the next few pages, then, are four of my short stories, with a few pertinent comments (or impertinent comments) about each.

In the late 1950s, in my pre-teen years, I worked at a sheep station in a remote section of Queensland, Australia. When the day's work was done, there were very few entertainment options for the shearers and other labourers. But one night there was great excitement because a visitor had arrived with some 'flickies'. Two of the shearing-wives tacked a bedsheet onto a wall, while the visitor set up a wondrous contraption which I'd never seen before: *a movie projector*. The moving-picture man had no audio system for his projector, so his cinematic selections consisted entirely of antique silent films with intertitles. That night, in a dimly-lit hut that smelt of lanolin and tar, I saw movies for the first time in my life.

Because all the films which I saw in my first night-at-the-movies were silent, I assumed that movies were *supposed* to be silent. I still haven't entirely changed my opinion on that subject. I am possibly the last living person who perceives *silent* films as the true version of the art form, and talking pictures as an embellishment. The silent movies which I saw that night included a slapstick comedy, a costume melodrama, and a film which featured a mob of hysterical thespians all desperately overacting while — in the midst of their histrionics — one quietly persuasive actor spoke eloquently without uttering a sound. That actor's name was Lon Chaney . . . and he remains the greatest actor I have ever seen.

'An Actor Prepares' is my homage to Lon Chaney. It's also one of my rare attempts to write fiction from a *female* viewpoint. I wrote this story for *Albedo*, a magazine published in Ireland which offers some of the most imaginative science fiction and fantasy of recent years. Because the narrator of this story has a European viewpoint — and because this story was originally published in Ireland — I've used standard British syntax and spelling in 'An Actor Prepares' . . . except for Lon Chaney's dialogue, which I've intentionally rendered in 1920s Yankspeak since Chaney was American. This may have been confusing for *Albedo*'s typesetters, because their published version of this story contained so many typos that some parts of it were rendered nearly incomprehensible. For example, the phrase 'legless criminal' was typographically glitched into 'legalised criminal' . . . whatever *that's* supposed to mean.

Here, then — for the first time as it was *originally* written — is my tribute to the Man of a Thousand Faces.

AN ACTOR PREPARES

Originally published in *Albedo #20*, 1999.

I had to appear when I was summoned; that is one of the rules which governs our domain. It is not widely known among the living that my people can teleport . . . yet we *can*, within our undead limitations.

A moment before, I had slept in my unhallowed bed; now I found myself, of a sudden, standing erect within a hastily-scribed chalk circle bearing the necessary symbols and sigils.

"You look well, gentle Ingra," said a long-familiar voice, and — although I have not breathed for three centuries — I exhaled a sigh of relief. It was Christensen who had summoned me: a dear friend and sweet comrade. He stepped forward, careful not to place any portion of himself within the profane circle. "Thank you for coming on such short notice," he smirked, knowing full well that I had been given no choice in the matter.

I found myself in curious surroundings. There were walls here, yet the walls were merely painted canvas stretched across wooden frameworks. *Liars' walls.* "What is this place to which you summon me?" I asked.

Benjamin Christensen was tall, blond, and grinning; I would gladly have bitten the smirk from his face . . . but, as he was the summoner and I the summoned, it was *he* and not I who held the power here. "I have brought you, sweet Ingra," he said in his thick Danish accent, "to a place called California. To be precise: we are on a movie set, in a city named Hollywood, in a make-believe land known as the Metro-Goldwyn-Mayer Studios. The local time is twelve minutes past midnight. Which means that there is now full daylight in the region of Europe from which I summoned your unliving essence."

He waved one hand while grinning innocently. I have often noticed that, if he were stripped naked and shorn of his body hair, Benjamin Christensen might easily pass for a cherub. Yet he is the only cherub whom I have seen dancing skyclad at Black Masses in Stockholm and Berlin. My summoner Christensen is four-square a disciple of Satan, despite the fact that his own surname begins with the name of our Rival.

I inspected the surroundings warily. "How long since last I awakened?"

"Not long," said Christensen. "During the recent Great War, I recall, after you drank the blood of so many gallant young soldiers and virile *poilus* in Ardennes and the Somme, you vowed that you would sleep for at least seven years. It has been *eight* years since we last crossed paths, gentle Ingra, and, if you will forgive me for citing the calendar which our opponents use, . . ." — he shuddered delicately — ". . . today is the morning of June twenty-eighth, in the year of *their* Lord, 1927." Christensen extended his hand. "Come, my dear. I desire that you would meet a friend of mine."

"Is he a disciple of our craft?" I inquired.

"Alas, no. Yet he is an artist whose skill I respect . . . and I can pay no higher compliment." Christensen took my arm, thereby allowing my undead essence to solidify more rapidly, and I stepped out of the cabalistic circle which he had chalked on the floor. "Let nothing surprise you in this place," Christensen whispered as he ushered me through a doorway.

We entered a corridor that seemed to border several centuries at once, for — as we traversed it — I saw male and female refugees from all known times and histories: Cossack soldiers and Babylonian courtesans, Tudor peasants and fur-clad Neanderthals, as well as aviators from the recent Great War.

Christensen saw my astonishment, and his belly shook mirthfully. "These people are *extras*, my dear. In costume for various crowd scenes. Night filming, you see."

Two scantily-skirted young females approached us. Their kneecaps were rouged, and one woman's hair was an unlikely shade of yellow. Both females gaped at the burial garments which I am required to wear, and then one woman nudged the other. "Pipe the glad rags on *her*," she sneered, nodding at me while her jaws chewed a wad of some glutinous substance. Both women giggled and kept walking. They looked too pale and anaemic to merit my attentions.

Christensen's blue eyes twinkled with glee. "Sweet Ingra, those two flappers mistook you for an actress in costume. I wish that your exquisite features were capable of being photographed: Theda Bara and Pola Negri would have to look to their laurels, and you would be — quite literally — the greatest *vampire* on the silver screen."

I shuddered when Christensen mentioned *silver*. "What devil-capers have you been up to since last we met?" I asked my summoner.

Benjamin Christensen's massive chest swelled to even larger proportions as he boasted: "In Copenhagen, after the Armistice, I filmed an actual Black Mass. I included the footage in a movie which I called *Häxan — The Witches* — although it is perhaps more notoriously known as *Witchcraft Through the Ages*. A mere trifle, yet it spawned a sensation in cinemas throughout Europe and America. Thus I am now ensconced as a film director here in Hollywood, where money flows freely and there are many handsome young men who share my — *ahem!* — esoteric interests."

We passed out of doors now, to a row of vehicles resembling Gypsy caravans, which Christensen informed me were called *trailers*. "The man whom I wish you to meet is here," said my summoner, bringing me to the threshold of a trailer far less gaudy than its brethren. Above the entrance, a hand-lettered card displayed a brief name: **LON CHANEY**.

"You may feel quite at ease," said Christensen. "Mister Chaney is both an artist and a gentleman. Furthermore, he is expecting you. I shall leave the two of you alone to discuss Undeath and Art and other sacrileges." Christensen's hand rapped once, twice upon the trailer's wooden door. Then he turned and strode away from me, towards a distant building which bore a sign marked COMMISSARY.

From inside the trailer, a baritone voice spoke: *"Come in."*

So I came *through* the door, in the same way that I once crossed through the portal named Death. I ceased to exist on *this* side, and my shattered essence rejoined on the distant side.

I stood in a room of modest furnishings, with a table and two chairs. On the table was a brown leather box marked L. CHANEY. Its lid was raised, and inside the box were faces: eyes, noses, teeth, hair.

A man five feet nine inches tall sat mournfully in a chair. He wore a dressing-gown and some sort of American garment to cover his genitals; that was all. His soul, I perceived, was forty-four years long. His eyes were deep brown behind horn-rimmed glasses. His hair was short-cropped. His ears protruded from the sides of his head like the handles of a coffin. Two small moles, one above the other, adorned his creased left cheek.

I am, of necessity, something of a connoisseur of teeth: Chaney's upper row of teeth were straight, but his bottom row were as jumble-crooked as neglected tombstones. A collection of scars were displayed on various regions of his body. The deepest scars he wore were on his soul.

The man named Chaney displayed no surprise as I came through the door in vapoured form and recorporated myself inside his trailer. *"Huh!* A pretty good trick," he said, rubbing his chin with his knuckles. "A reverse fade-away. I wish I could have pulled that stunt when I toured with Fischer's Follies back in '12. It would have helped me get away from an angry audience. You must be Miss Ingra. Please have a seat."

I did not sit. There was a mirror on the dressing-table. Chaney saw that the mirror displeased me, and he hastily covered it with a towel. Now I asked him: "You have been told who I am? *What* I am?"

"Yes, yes. Of course. Christensen told me." Chaney rubbed his hands together eagerly. "Want something to eat? Maybe a drink?"

"Perhaps I may partake *later,*" I said.

"Oh. I get you, kid. Christensen told me that you people — *nosferatu,* is that the word? — never eat anything. That's the bunk, and Christensen can go tell it to Sweeney; everybody eats *something*. Of course you know why you're here?"

I lowered my eyelids disdainfully. "I was summoned. I had no choice but to come."

"And Christensen didn't tell you *why?* That Danish bohunk!" Chaney jumped up and paced the small room. "All right, it's like this: I'm an actor. Maybe you've seen my movies when you . . . uh, no; I guess you don't get out much." Suddenly Chaney's head jerked backwards on his neck reflexively; he ignored this, and thrust an unlit cigarette into his mouth. "You mind if I smoke, Miss?"

"Smoke and I are old friends," I replied. "Please tell me why I am here."

"Christensen brought you here as a favor to me," Chaney said through a mouthful of cigarette as he lit it. "Have a look at these." From a drawer in his table he took a black leather notebook, and opened it.

The book was full of faces. Photographic portraits of dozens of men. Then, as I turned the pages, it occurred to me that all the men wihtin these photographs were Chaney. By some unknown alchemy, he had altered his features in an astonishing number of ways to form these likenesses. He stood behind me now, keeping up a rapid narrative, as I examined his faces: "That one there, see? That's when I played Fagin in *Oliver Twist*. He was easy to do; I just read the book and copied the description. Same deal when I played Quasimodo in *Hunchback of Notre Dame*. Pipe this mug here, see him? Then I had to play a sailor in *All the Brothers Were Valiant*, so I went down to the Merchant Hall and

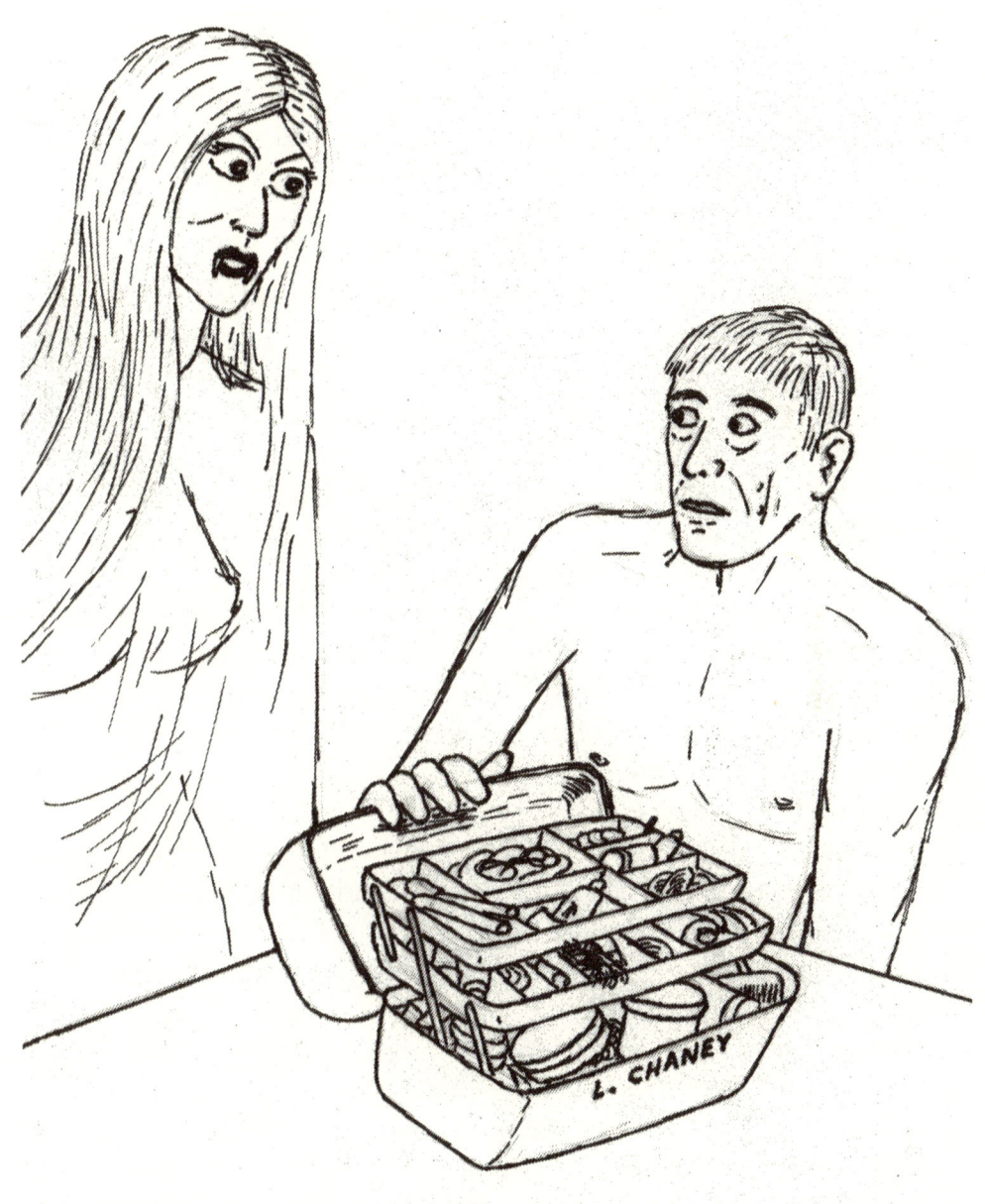

Gwynplaine

L. CHANEY

I studied sailors till I had the role down. Then I was cast as a drill sergeant in *Tell It to the Marines*, so I just went to the Marine base at San Diego and made a regular nuisance of myself." Chaney grinned at the memory; his smile was easy and engaging.

I did not feel like smiling; I was half a world away from my coffined remains . . . and the longer I sustained my essence here, the greater was the strain on my unsoul. "What has any of this to do with *me*, please?" I asked him.

Chaney sat in a chair and crossed his legs; once, twice over themselves, so that his right foot locked grotesquely behind his left ankle. "I've just wrapped a film here at Metro that Ben Christensen directed," Chaney told me. "The film's called *Mockery*. I play a Russian peasant during the revolution. I've never been to Russia, but Thalberg was savvy enough to find some Russians who skedaddled out of Moscow one jump ahead of the Bolsheviks. They've been over here long enough to speak English. So I climbed into my role by studying them. Miss Ingra, I'm very careful that my portrayals are always accurate. Genuine sailors. Official U.S. Marines. Authentic Russians. Whenever I lend my flesh to a character, I always study someone who *is* that character."

The actor named Chaney sat silently for a moment, inhaling the smoke of his cigarette. Now he went on: "I've just been handed the shooting script for my next film. Tod Browning will direct it. The working title is either *The Hypnotist* or *London After Midnight*. Miss Ingra, in this movie I'll be playing two roles . . . and one of them is a vampire."

I said nothing.

"You see my problem, of course," Chaney went on. "To prepare for this role, I've got to pick the brains of a vampire. Christensen likes to spout off about witchcraft and hexes, so just for a razz I asked him: 'Got any vampires handy?' When he said yes, I thought he was joking; now I find out he had the McCoy."

"There is nothing of jokes in my people," I said. "What is it that you desire of me?"

"Everything," said Chaney. "All of it. How it feels to be a vampire. What do you *do*? What do you *want*? Does a vampire have dreams? Does a vampire have *nightmares*? Show me the country that lies beyond Death. Tell me what you are, and what you were, and hope to be."

He exhaled a double lungful of smoke, and then I gave my reply: "Such knowledge is not given freely, Mister Chaney. I will require . . . an *exchange*."

86

"Natch. Of course. Money? I'll write you a check. Or maybe you'd prefer . . ." He broke off, as my eyes reached out and found his own eyes in the silence. He saw the answer in my eyes, and then he knew.

"A few minutes ago," I told him, "you were kind enough to offer me a drink. I will have that drink now, if you please."

Chaney's hand crept nervously to his throat.

"No, not *there*," I assured him. "That would make you one of us, and he who summoned me here has forbidden me to conscript you. Somewhere else."

Chaney's body was a network of scars. Now he fingered a dark blemish on his left thigh. "Maybe there?" he asked me. "That's where I broke a vein, strapping my ankles back behind my thighs, when I played the legless criminal in *The Penalty*. Or how's about here?" He rolled up his sleeve, and showed me a similar discoloration on his right arm. "I had my arms strapped up tight against my ribs for hours, when I played a man with no arms in *The Unknown*. You want a piece of my back? The old spine hasn't been right since I played Quasimodo." Chaney's head jerked backward spasmodically; the same gesture I'd observed before. "Or will this cost me an eye? I've played so many blind men and Chinese parts, my eyelids are shot. For the close-ups in *Phantom of the Opera*, I wired my eye sockets with . . ."

I interrupted his litany. "Please. Give me your hand."

"Which one?" Chaney lifted his right hand, then reconsidered. "No, better not; I'm right-handed." He offered me his left hand. "Don't mind the scar on my palm; I got that in my barnstorming days when an actress accidentally shot me onstage during a mellerdrammer. The audience thought it was part of . . ."

"Please." I took his hand, and raised it toward my mouth. Then . . . as always, as ever, I *bit*. And I drank.

The blood was sweet yet bitter. I drank his disappointments, and I fed on his triumphs. His blood was hot with his passions: the passions of an artist who sculpted his creations in his own flesh for the cameras. I tasted his past: his first wife who had betrayed him, his son who had disappointed him. The younger brother who had died in infancy, and the parents — both of them deaf-mutes — who had spent their lives in silent isolation. All the threads in the tapestry of his soul. All, *all*, I tasted and took.

Afterwards, I wiped my lips daintily on the towel he offered me. "You have paid well," I nodded. "Now it is time for me to impart the knowledge which you requested. Gaze into my eyes."

The cigarette fell, silently, from Chaney's paled lips. My eyes tasted his own. And now I gave.

I did not speak, and yet I *told*. I told him all of the Undeath. How it begins. How it sustains itself. The stirrings that I feel within my dead immortal flesh when sunset comes and darkness beckons. The bottomless craving. The blood. Always first, there is blood: first and last and eternal. I told him how I taste the fear of my prey, and how that fear sweetens and ripens the blood in their veins as I drink. I told all. I told secrets unspoken. In the dark of that room, I divulged the Undeath.

Chaney was silent for a long while after I finished. Then he noticed, as if for the first time, the two puncture wounds in the palm of his left hand. He found something in a first-aid kid, pressed it to his bloodied hand. "Thank you, Miss," he whispered. "That's all I . . . all I wanted to know."

I had fulfilled my summoner's task; now I was impatient to step into the circle again, so that I could rejoin my absent body. I departed from Chaney's presence; I vapoured myself through the door, and went out.

As my essence reformed on the other side, a man approached. By his uniform, I knew him for a watchman or a security guard. He saw my shrouded garments, and he spoke to me: "No costumes to be taken off the lot, sister. Get those duds back to Wardrobe, quick."

I pushed past the gendarme, and strode onward down the corridor. "I am no mere actress," I told him disdainfully.

"No kidding?" The guard sounded suspicious, and he followed me as I went back to the pattern of symbols which Christensen had drawn. "Which production are you with?" the guard demanded.

"*London After Midnight*, starring Lon Chaney," I answered.

The guard came after me as I stepped into the circle. "That movie won't start filming until late July," he persisted. "What's yer job title, then: Script girl? Make-up? Continuity?"

"*Technical advisor,*" I said. And then I vanished.

'Marooned Off Pallas' has never been published before. I wrote it during the last months of the year 2000, on the brink of the new millennium, and I decided to include the story in this anthology. I got the idea for it after re-reading an old favourite: 'Marooned Off Vesta', a 1939 space-opera epic which happens to be the first published story written by Isaac Asimov.

I try to create fiction that's as accurate as possible. Several authors have written stories taking place inside the asteroid belt between Mars and Jupiter, but — so far as I know — my 'Marooned Off Pallas' is the very first story ever to utilise specific *real-life* features of that region. The places which I mention in this story — the Koronis zone, the Hungarias zone and so forth — are all authentic portions of our solar system's asteroid belt. I predict that the Kirkwood gaps will become important places in the twenty-first and twenty-second centuries, as we begin colonising our neighbouring planets.

I also predict that American explorers and American technology will lead the way to those worlds, which is why I've used Yankspeak idioms and dialogue in the following story.

I expect that some readers will complain about the female mission specialist in this story: I will stand accused of creating a character who is a stereotype rather than a flesh-and-blood human. In self-defence, I'll point out that some people really *do* conform to stereotypes: usually the people who let Political Correctness dictate their actions and their priorities. I hope that Political Correctness will die a well-deserved death before we colonise the Moon and Mars.

And, on that cheerful thought, I give you 'Marooned Off Pallas'.

MAROONED
OFF PALLAS

I wasn't expecting an asteroid, but I was heading for a collision with *something* when Fleet Command teamed me with a mission specialist named Lilith Virago.

Yes, damn her: Lilith Virago. She claimed it was her real name, and I don't have access to the Fleet's personnel files, so I'll take her word for it. I couldn't accuse her of false advertising: she had *exactly* the kind of personality to go with a name like Lilith Virago.

When I told her that I pilot a two-man shuttlecraft, Lilith Virago replied that it was a two-*person* vessel, thank you very much. She also warned me that she would file a charge of sexual harassment if I ever dared refer to her as my ship*mate*. Then she pointed out that women are better qualified for spaceflight than men are: on deep-space assignments, female-crewed missions require less oxygen than men would use. Women also require less water, less food, less life-support . . . and therefore ships with all-female crews carry a more efficient payload than spaceships crewed by males.

Well, excuse me for having a Y-chromosome, and the gonads that come with it. The laws of biology give female spacemen — I mean, female space*persons* — a slight career edge over me and every other male, but I've never let my gender compromise my ambition. I was born and raised in one of the early Luna colonies: ever since I saw my first Earthrise in the night sky over my boyhood home in Tycho City, all I've ever wanted was to live and work in outer space.

If it were the other way around — if men were better designed for spaceflight than women are — I would never use that as an excuse to exclude women from the Fleet. My service record proves that I've never had any problem serving alongside female officers, or taking orders from women who outrank me. No problem, that is, until Fleet Command issued orders to mission-team me with Lilith Virago, postmodern radical feminist and intergalactic lesbian. If it were up to *her*, outer space would be a clubhouse for women only, with a sign reading NO BOYS ALLOWED.

During our first mission briefing, she insisted that I address her as "Ms. Virago". I outrank her by half a duty grade, so I've called her "Lilith" ever since, just to annoy her. Rank has its privileges.

Anyway, the asteroid.

We were assigned to a surveying run across the central subdivisions of the asteroid belt between Mars and Jupiter: specifically, I was supposed to bring our shuttlecraft across a long arc between the asteroid belt's Phocaeas zone and Themis zone, while Lilith charted those regions and scanned the local 'roids for mineral deposits or water ice that could be used by the Luna colonists. Afterwards, we were scheduled to rendezvous with our command ship, the *Sagan*, inside the Koronis zone: a deeper region of the asteroid belt.

Somehow, during the surveying run, Lilith and I got into an argument on her favorite subject — the innate superiority of the female versus the male — and we fell behind schedule. I knew we'd never make an on-time rendezvous with the *Sagan* . . . at least, not if we took Fleet Command's assigned route to get there.

All authorized Fleet routes through the asteroid belt use the Kirkwood gaps. Over the past four billion years, the powerful gravity well of the planet Jupiter has cleared all the debris out of several regions of the asteroid belt that are harmonic factors of Jupiter's orbital period. The Kirkwood gaps have orbital periods exactly equal to one-fourth, one-third, three-sevenths, and one-half of Jupiter's cycle . . . so whenever I set course through those gaps in the asteroid belt, I can lay down some speed without bothering to watch for interplanetary boulders crossing my flight path.

But the regions of space *between* the Kirkwoods are chock-full of navigational hazards. To reach our rendezvous point in the Koronis zone, I would have to alternate between high-speed intervals of clear sailing and slow crawls through asteroid minefields. To hell with that. Against orders, I charted a route that would get us to the rendezvous much faster, by flying thirty degrees out of the ecliptic . . . and not returning to the ecliptic until we approached the 'roid belt's Koronis subdivision.

It worked just dandy. My unauthorized course took our shuttlecraft clear out of the asteroid belt's orbital plane and into a trajectory with no space debris at all. I unthrottled the drive, and we traveled full speed . . . *slam into an asteroid.*

One damn dumb puny little asteroid, in a rogue orbit outside the main asteroid belt. One tiny microlith; more like a footnote than a full-fledged asteroid. An asteroid asterisk. The damned space-pebble penetrated our hull *twice* — coming in, and going out again — and suddenly our shuttlecraft was leaking oxygen.

Lilith and I initiated emergency hull-breach procedures, bringing the auxiliary hull plates on-line before we lost too much air. The ship was knocked galley-west by our impact with the microlith, but I was too busy helping Lilith seal the hull breach to find out where we were going. I'm a trained pilot: when the ship goes off course, my gut call is to ignore everything else and correct the helm. But we were leaking oxygen rapidly: I had to grit my teeth and override my instincts, letting the shuttle careen blindly through interplanetary space while Lilith and I gave full priority to sealing the hull breaches. We weren't likely to slam into any random space-flotsam a *second* time; technically we were still inside the asteroid belt, but we were so far off the main ecliptic that there weren't many navigational hazards.

Finally, after the auxiliary hull plates were unshipped and secured, I caught my breath — grateful that I still had an onboard air supply to catch my breath *with* — and I took the helm bearings. Then I made a status check, all systems . . . and that's when I found out just how deeply we were trapped in double doo-doo.

The Ops readouts showed several tiny hull fractures. We couldn't pinpoint their locations, because the ship's internal sensors were damaged. The fractures were small enough to be invisible, but large enough to do their deadly work: we were slowly leaking oxygen, leaking heat, leaking fuel.

The hull section containing our water tank had been gutted, and our water supply was lost. By dumb luck, I had gulped down a large drink of water just a few minutes before the disaster struck; whatever else happened, I wouldn't die of thirst.

Worse luck: the microlith had punctured one of our power couplings, causing a massive surge that fried most of our primary systems. When I saw the damage, I knew we were doomed.

Our communications system was bollixed; the transceivers were futtbucked beyond all redemption. We couldn't transmit a wideband SOS to the *Sagan* or anyone else. We still had the two-way comlinks in the EVA rigs of our spacesuits, but those were strictly for short-range messages during extra-vehicular activity. We had no way to boost the comlinks' transmission range far enough to call for help.

Worst of all: our navigation and propulsion systems were DOA. We were dead in the water . . . and with no water in our shattered water tank, that left us nothing but *dead*.

When Lilith and I finally brought the ship's external sensors back on-line, the first thing we saw outside our viewports was one big-ass asteroid. The sensors ID'd the rock for us. It was Pallas: the second-largest asteroid in the solar system, and — with an orbital inclination of 34.8 degrees — the only major asteroid that deviates significantly from the ecliptic. Which meant that *nobody was likely to find us.*

Fleet pilots have standing orders to keep all vessels within ±10 degrees of the ecliptic. When a Fleet ship disappears, those are the maximum vectors for a standard search protocol. But my unauthorized short-cut had taken us far outside the search vectors. If Pallas was on the high end of its orbit — near aphelion — then our shuttle was farther beyond the ecliptic than the *Sagan* or any other Fleet vessel was ever likely to come looking for us.

In other words, we were dead. Not yet, but any time now.

*   *   *

The goddess of Wisdom kept thumbing her nose at me, each time my viewport passed her cratered face. Pallas is nearly spherical: it's one of the very few asteroids with enough gravitational mass to sculpt its component matter into a compact ball. A *dark gray* ball: nearly black, because Pallas is mostly basaltic achondrite. But there was one large white outcropping of raw magnesium sulfate, jutting erect from the cratered sphere like the beak of a vulture. Or the upraised snoot of a disdainful goddess, staring down her nose at me. Some nineteenth-century joker had named this chunk of flying real estate *Pallas*, after the ancient goddess of Wisdom. But there wasn't much wisdom — or anything else I could use — in the cold landscape outside my viewport: just the shadow of our crippled shuttlecraft, tumbling in orbit above the asteroid.

The magnesium sulfate field was on the daylight side of Pallas, so — each time our orbit brought us to that side of the asteroid — I could see the shadow of our shuttlecraft far below, on the asteroid's surface. Each time we made an orbital transit, the shuttle's shadow briefly wrinkled and flexed across the white hill of magnesium crystals . . . then abruptly straightened again. As if the goddess of Wisdom had placed her thumb against her nose and waggled her fingers in a mongrel salute whenever I sailed overhead.

93

An asteroid was giving me the finger.

From some long-ago Biochem class, I suddenly recalled that magnesium sulfate is the basic ingredient in Epsom salt. Well, now I had a whole mountain of the stuff — right outside my viewport, just out of reach — but it couldn't cure the headache I had. My skull felt like it wanted to secede from my spinal column and set up its own independent republic. I knew that my headache would feel even worse soon, when the oxygen began to fail . . .

"Will you please stop walking up and down like that?" said Lilith Virago, glaring at me from her chair at the Mission console, while I walked across the starboard bulkhead. "If you *must* pace back and forth, you could at least align your body axis with the compartment."

I had no sympathy for most of Ms. Virago's complaints, but this time she was right. From her viewpoint, I was standing on a wall and projecting sideways across her field of vision. I've logged enough hours in microgravity to know how spacesick it can feel when somebody else's rightside up is your upside down.

I walked down the bulkhead and squatted near the implosion site that used to be our Navigation console. "I'm trying to think of a way out of this deathtrap," I told Lilith, pretending not to notice her anger. "If *you've* got any ideas, feel free to speak up."

"Me? *I'm* not the one who got us into this mess," she parried. *"You* did this. As usual, a typical *male* is too conceited to stop and ask for directions!"

There are times when I'd like to strangle Lilith Virago, and there are other times when I just want to flush her out into space and let the infinite void of the cosmos take its chances with her. Just now she was even more insufferable than usual, because she was absolutely right: this crisis was entirely *my* fault. If I'd consulted the navigational sensors — if I'd bothered to "ask for directions" before setting a course off-ecliptic — I would have spotted that microlith before it punched through our hull. But I hadn't, so it did and we were doomed. For whatever it was worth, Ms. Virago was entitled to laugh herself sick over my macho mistake . . . until our dwindling air supply would leave her with nothing to laugh at. Or with.

We had one chance to save our hides. Nine years ago, when our probe ships first started prospecting the 'roid belt, Fleet Command placed emergency supply depots on each of the ten largest asteroids: distress beacons, power packs, spare tanks of oxygen. None of these had ever been used,

94

because no other Fleet pilot had ever pulled a bone-headed stunt like mine . . . but the supply depots were still inspected and maintained on a yearly basis, in case they were ever needed. I sure as hell needed one *now*. If I could land our crippled shuttle on Pallas, somewhere on that cratered basalt surface was a beacon that I could activate, to call for help . . . and the provisions that would keep Lilith and me alive for a few more hours.

Yeah. Somewhere. But *where?* The Ops readouts told me that Pallas is just a skoonch less than 539 kilometers wide. I did a rapid calculation in my head, pretending that $\pi = 3$ so that I could avoid fractions . . . *damn!* According to my math, the surface area of Pallas is roughly *913,000 square kilometers.* Pretty damned big for an asteroid. And there was only *one* supply depot, somewhere among all those craters. Even if I could somehow land our damaged shuttle on the asteroid's surface — with no propulsion system, and no guidance array — the odds were 913,000 to one against us landing within a spacewalk's distance of the one precious supply depot on Pallas.

Just as I thought of this, something white — that outcropping of magnesium sulfate — flicked past my viewport again, and once more the goddess of Wisdom thumbed her nose at me. We weren't getting any closer to Pallas. I checked the Ops board: that collision with the microlith had knocked our shuttle into a parking orbit, about 350 kilometers above the asteroid. I kept hoping our orbit would decay slightly . . . just enough to bring us into a spiraling descent, so that I could scan the surface of Pallas for that supply depot.

No good. I used what was left of our navigational software to double-check the shuttle's trajectory. By some damned fluke, our shuttle was trapped in a *stable* orbit over Pallas, almost perfectly circular. Never getting any closer to that distress beacon. And never getting any nearer to a standard Fleet search vector.

Now that we were caught in the asteroid's gravity well, Lilith and I and our damaged shuttle had shifted from microgravity into minigravity. Across my body, I felt the inner layer of my spacesuit ripple and shift as the liquid coolant beneath my exosuit readjusted itself within its network of tubes, flowing away from my shoulders and towards my chest and my legs: the regions of my body that were slightly closer to Pallas. At least now there was a definite *downwards* . . . but no way for us to get down to where the supply depot was.

I had a desperate idea. I could suit up, put on my helmet and EVA rig, and go out the airlock. In minigravity, my escape velocity would be nearly zero. One good kick against the shuttle's outer hull would generate enough kinetic energy to propel me away from the ship and send me plummeting freefall — in ultra-slow motion — down to the asteroid's surface.

Damn it, *no*. No good at all. I would have no way to steer, no chance for a course correction. If I kicked off at *precisely* the correct tangent, I would propel myself into a slow-motion plunge towards Pallas . . . with no guarantee that I would land anywhere near the distress beacon, and almost a certainty that my spacesuit would run out of oxygen during the slo-mo descent. But if I kicked off from the hull at any one of an infinite number of *wrong* tangents, with no guidance system, I would drift helplessly into space with no chance of . . .

Suddenly, my bladder twinged; I'd taken that long drink of water just before we lost our water tank, and now I felt an urge to relieve myself. I crossed the shuttle's habitat section and I did a damage-check of our onboard latrine. *In space, nobody can hear you flush* . . . but Lilith Virago has given me plenty of grief over our standard Fleet-issue unisex micrograv toilet. In outer space, there is no "up" or "down" . . . and yet I have to share a zero-gravity toilet with a woman who complains if I leave the seat *up*.

The shuttle's toilet wasn't damaged. It was designed to work in every condition from Earth-normal gravity to zero-gee; it has a swivel-mounted airflow duct that can treat any direction as "down", flushing away waste products and freeze-drying them for disposal later. Now I opened the hatchway to the toilet stall, intending to use the facilities . . . until I had a sudden morbid thought: any minute now, when the shuttle's air supply got close to zero, Lilith and I might need to cannibalize the toilet's airflow cartridge to prolong our dwindling oxygen supply. If we didn't use the micrograv toilet for its intended function, we might buy a few minutes' survival time. I would have to face death with a full bladder.

I started thinking out loud, desperate for an idea. "Something in this set-up seems familiar," I told Lilith. "I remember reading something similar, about somebody trapped in orbit above an asteroid . . ."

"You must be mistaken, *as usual*," she sniffed. "There's no such text in Fleet archives. There *can't* be. Until *now*, no Fleet vessel has ever been trapped in . . ."

Suddenly an alarm went off, near the portside nacelle. A sensor relay was overloading! Lilith's long spacesuited legs kicked off against the deckplates, sending her cartwheeling through minigravity with feline grace, across the habitat section and towards the port nacelle. But I had kicked off, too, and my *male* limbs had a double advantage: since my legs were longer than Lilith's, I had greater leverage . . . powered by larger quantities of muscle mass. I sailed past Lilith in midair — exceeding her velocity, but with a technique that was closer to ursine than feline — and I reached the nacelle overload several seconds ahead of her.

No time to lose. I tore off the panel housing and shoved my right arm down the shaft of the relay conduit, feeling for the emergency cut-off. *Damn!* The switch was fused. I could bypass it, but I would need both hands down there at the bottom of the conduit, to disengage the microchips from the circuit board underneath where the switch used to be. Quickly, I withdrew my right arm halfway from the relay conduit, slipping my left hand halfway down the narrow shaft alongside my right arm.

Both arms wouldn't fit. The conduit was wide enough to hold either one of my arms . . . but not *both*, and this was a two-handed job. How could . . .

"Get out of my way, please." Quickly, calmly, Lilith Virago lifted me bodily and moved me away from the panel. I outweighed her, but in minigravity it barely made a difference.

I watched from the sidelines, impotently, as Mission Specialist Virago slipped both of her thin arms down the conduit. My male arms were longer than hers, but Lilith's female physique had the design advantage: her narrow shoulders enabled her to bring her forearms closer together — nearly parallel — so that both of her hands worked in tandem inside the cramped workspace. She did something that made the alarm change its pitch; I couldn't see Lilith's hands, but I envisioned her long tapering female fingers gripping some mechanism that my stubbier male digits couldn't have reached. Now the alarm went silent, and Lilith smiled triumphantly. Her arms were halfway inside the shaft, so close together that her elbows actually *touched* inside the narrow workspace. Most women can touch their elbows together, or pretty close. But men can't do it: male shoulders are too far apart for that.

The shuttle's relay conduits weren't *designed* to accommodate male forearms; under normal field conditions, the shuttle relays never malfunctioned in any manner requiring that particular access. But this time they *had* . . . and Lilith Virago fixed the damage easily, in a place where my wide shoulders and bulky forearms couldn't even reach.

Lilith cleaned her hands on a workwipe. She saw me looking at my own

97

brawny arms, and she flashed that smug radical-feminist grin of hers that I can see coming from a parsec away. "Further proof of what I keep telling you," she smirked. "The male anatomy is less efficiently designed than the female anatomy, for every possible task . . . *except* brute strength. But in outer space, brute strength is useless: in microgravity, everything is weightless." Her face had an expression of mock pity. "Maybe back on Earth there are still a few job opportunities for steroid jocks who majored in bench-pressing . . . but interplanetary space is definitely a *female* realm."

It was typical of this woman that she would lecture me even while our lives were at stake. This was a time to be thinking about asteroids, not steroids. Lilith had fixed the immediate crisis of the sensor overload, but we were still marooned off Pallas, facing slow death, with no . . .

Suddenly I remembered. *"Now* I know where it was," I told Lilith. "I *did* read about a situation like this. Three men in a damaged ship, trapped in orbit above an asteroid. Only it wasn't Pallas."

Lilith's mouth tightened. "You couldn't have read it, because this situation has never happened before."

"No, it wasn't in Fleet records. This was *fiction*, I think." I went to the Operations console, muttering a silent prayer that the ship's computer archives would still be on-line, so that I could access the file I needed. I wasn't sure of where to find it, so I keyed in a search-directory command and held my breath.

Ever since the Möbius chip was invented in 2043, we've made tremendous strides in data storage, so that now even the onboard computer of a two-man . . . sorry; a two-*person* space shuttle can archive billions of bytes in a buttonhole's worth of storage space. Senior-grade Fleet officers on deep-space duty are permitted fifty terabytes in our ships' computer archives for personal use; there's so damned much room in the database, Fleet Command can afford to be generous. Before our shuttle left Luna, I'd downloaded enough text files of reading matter to keep myself busy for the next . . .

Click. There it was. I slid over, so that Lilith could see the text on the Ops monitor. "That's it," I told her. " 'Marooned Off Vesta'. A fictional narrative, originally published in . . ." — I squinted to read the smaller text window beside the main document — ". . . the March 1939 issue of *Amazing Stories*. Written by Isaac Asimov."

Lilith Virago yawned. "Isaac *who?*" she asked.

Oh, that's right; I forgot. My politically-correct crewmate has an encyclopedic knowledge of every Third World pagan earth-mother lesbian poetess who ever squatted in the mud and scratched sapphic screeds on tree-bark . . . but authors who lack vaginas don't merit inclusion in Lilith Virago's literary pantheon. "Don't pretend you never heard of Isaac Asimov," I said to her. "He was one of last century's most important authors."

"Important by *white male* standards, perhaps." Lilith yawned again. "Those of us who are *non-phallocentric* have our own standards of . . ."

"Are you going to keep playing that same broken disc-drive, or do you want us to get out of here alive?" I interrupted her. "I remember reading 'Marooned Off Vesta' years ago, in one of Asimov's anthologies. Something tells me there's a clue in here; something that can help us get out of this deathtrap."

"Well, since we're doomed anyway, and have no other options . . . ," Lilith's voice trailed off, and she slid into the seat next to me while I speed-scanned the text on my monitor.

Boyhood memories came flooding back to me: sitting in the school library at Tycho City, hunched over a monitor while I read this story for the first time. Now, fifteen years later, I read it again.

"Marooned Off Vesta" came amazingly close to predicting the deadly predicament that Lilith and I were in. Asimov's castaways were three males, but — just like us — their ship was damaged in a collision with a minor asteroid. Just like us, they were knocked into stable orbit above a major asteroid: theirs was Vesta, the fourth largest object in the asteroid belt. Just like us, they found themselves trapped with a dwindling air supply, but they had a chance to survive if they could find some way to *land* on the asteroid. And just like us, their damaged ship had no propulsion or guidance systems. But I remembered that somehow they got home alive. *How?* I licked my lips nervously, and speed-scrolled the text to reach the ending . . .

When I got there, I groaned. Asimov's story was no help at all. By chance, his fictional crew were aboard a ship supplied with 750,000 cubic feet of water. (In the Fleet, we measure liquid in kiloliters . . . but that wasn't the problem.) One of Asimov's fictional spacemen suited up, went outside with his handy-dandy raygun, and blasted a hole in the ship's water tank. Sucked out into the vacuum of space, the water functioned as a powerful propellant that nudged Asimov's fictional spaceship out of orbit and brought the crew to a gentle landing on Vesta.

That wouldn't work for *us*. Our water supply was gone. And Fleet

Command doesn't equip us with rayguns or blaster pistols.

Worst of all, for my purposes: Asimov had populated his fictional Vesta with space colonies. His castaways only needed to make landfall — *anywhere* on the asteroid — and rescue was nearby. That didn't help me. I had to bring our shuttle down within a bare kilometer of the only supply depot on the surface of Pallas. Or die slowly.

Isaac Asimov couldn't save us. I'd gone up a blind alley, with time running out . . . and our air leaking out along with it.

Beside me, Lilith snorted in contempt. She was still reading Asimov's story, and I saw that she had input a text-search for female pronouns. "Typical macho crap!" she sneered. "All the characters in this story are resourceful courageous *males*. Spacemen armed with rayguns, which are obvious surrogates for every male's favorite weapon: his *penis*. In this entire narrative, *female* story elements appear only twice, both times as sexual stereotypes: the men refer to their ship as *'she'*, and they blame their predicament on a personified 'Fate' . . . which they perceive as a capricious *female*. Sexist bastards!"

"Don't judge Asimov by our modern twenty-first century rules," I said defensively. "He was more accurate than most of his contemporaries. Unlike most other fiction writers of his time, Isaac Asimov was a professional scientist, with academic credentials."

Lilith snorted again. "Really? You wouldn't know it from this story. His science is full of holes."

Despite the coolant in my environmental suit, I felt my skin flush; I hadn't read any of Asimov's work in many years, but he *had* been one of my boyhood idols, and I didn't intend to let Ms. Virago subject him to postmodern feminist deconstruction. "What's wrong with Asimov's science?" I asked warily.

"Look at this." Lilith back-scrolled the text of "Marooned Off Vesta" to a highlighted passage. "See? Your space-heroes are in a *very* large ship, designed for several dozen occupants. So how do they land on Vesta? All they do is nudge their spaceship out of orbit and let it fall to the asteroid's surface. They expect to make a nice safe landing because . . ." — Lilith bent forward, quoting Asimov's words off the monitor — ". . . the asteroid *'hasn't got enough gravity to crush a cream puff'*."

I groaned again, and I mentally kicked myself for missing a scientific error that Lilith Virago had spotted instantly.

Asimov's physics *didn't work:* yes, his fictional spaceship would weigh barely a microgram in the meager gravity well of an asteroid like Vesta. But the spaceship still possessed its full inertial *mass:* several *tons* of mass, judging from Asimov's description of the ship. That microgram of weight would slam into Vesta's surface with many *tons'* worth of inertia, and, well, . . . *ouch.*

"Give Asimov credit for *something*, at least," I told Lilith. "Look what he does here, at his story's climax. Asimov was smart enough to realize that water released into the vacuum of outer space would become *steam*, because the lack of air pressure lowers water's boiling point . . . and its sublimation point. In 1939, most fictioneers would have guessed wrong: they would have made the escaping water turn into a block of *ice*, just because outer space is *cold.*"

"And *none* of this," said Lilith Virago, with a voice far colder than the winds of Jupiter, "will get us back into Fleet space alive. Instead of revisiting your prepubescent schoolboy fantasies, I suggest that you help me find some way out of here, *if you can.*"

Damn her, she did it again. Underneath her sociopolitical agenda, Lilith Virago had a tendency to be absolutely right about everything that actually mattered . . . such as our lives and our declining oxygen supply. I had let myself get sidetracked by "Marooned Off Vesta" because I'd thought that Isaac Asimov's story might have a solution to our deadly problem. I *still* thought so, for some reason. Or was I just being stubbornly loyal to a boyhood idol whose antique tales had outlived their usefulness?

Lilith and I were stuck with the laws of physics, even if Asimov's story sidestepped them. *If* I had several thousand cubic feet of water — which I didn't — I could send our shuttle plunging towards Pallas. But *then* what? I had no means of *guiding* our descent, no way to steer us towards that one precious supply depot that was our only hope. Even if I brought our ship down within sight of the distress beacon, we were *still* doomed. I had no way to *brake* our descent. Our cramped shuttle packed several metric tons of mass. Plummeting through an asteroid's faint gravity well, the ship would weigh as little as a snowflake . . . but at the end of that plunge, our ship's inertial mass would catch up with us: *boom!*

At the Operations monitor, I stored the text of "Marooned Off Vesta" and I accessed the stats for the asteroid Pallas, in case there was some fluke in this 'roid's sidereal period or its orbital inclination that might save us. Now

I found something I hadn't known: even though Pallas is slightly larger than Vesta — about 16 kilometers wider — it actually has *less* gravity, because it has less density. According to my readouts, Vesta outweighs Pallas by three ten-billionths of a solar mass. In the gravity well of Pallas, our crippled shuttle was even lighter than I'd realized.

But so damned *what?* Weight and mass are two different things, even though we measure them in the same units. The tiniest nudge could drop our shuttle out of orbit: we weighed barely a microgram. But we would still slam into the basalt surface of Pallas with several metric *tons* of mass.

I was starting to feel desperate. "I still think that Asimov had the right idea," I told Lilith, ignoring her skeptical look. "But he used it the wrong way. Asimov's spaceman blasted a hole in a water tank, and let several tons of water escape. But he didn't *need* so much propellant; just a tiny amount, to nudge his ship towards Vesta, would have done the same job. And he had no way to *steer* that flow of water, or to alter velocity. If Asimov had put a *spigot* on his water tank, he could have guided his spaceship into a safe landing trajectory, despite its mass. Just aim the spigot's flow *above* the ship to begin a descent. Aim *ahead* of the ship to brake its descent, and then aim *beneath* the ship — like a retro-rocket — as it touches down for planetfall."

As usual, Lilith Virago looked unimpressed. "Congratulations," she said. "You've saved the lives of Asimov's fictional macho-men. But will this help *us* get out of here alive?"

"Maybe it can," I said, feeling a hunch coming. "We don't have tons of water, like Asimov's characters did, but we won't need that much." Now I was getting an idea. "Wait a minute! All we need is about a liter's worth of fluid . . . *under pressure*, so that it acts as a propellant. A liter's worth of fluid, in a pressurized container that vents through a spigot."

Lilith arched one eyebrow. "What *kind* of spigot?"

"A faucet that can turn on and off, with an adjustable flow." I was trying to visualize the gizmo while I described it. "Open the spigot full blast to brake our descent, or let it send out a faint drizzle for minor course corrections. A spigot that can aim in several different directions. It doesn't have to be large. In fact, a small spigot would be easier to control than a large one."

"That might work!" said Lilith, showing genuine enthusiasm. "But our shuttle isn't equipped for experiments in fluid dynamics. Where will we find this lucky spigot?"

"We'll have to jerry-rig one," I said. "Look, I really *can't* think about this right now." I glanced desperately towards the microgravity toilet. "My bladder's so full, it feels like it's about to burst its floodgates. I really *have* to take a . . ."

"That's it!" Lilith Virago was staring at me. Specifically, she was staring at the lower half of my spacesuit, and a portion of my male anatomy that had never previously aroused Lilith Virago's attention.

"You don't suppose . . .?" she wondered half-aloud.

"What are you talking about?" I asked.

Lilith Virago was staring at my crotch as if it offered the solution to all her problems. "One liter of fluid under intense pressure," she said. "Flowing out through a spigot that can aim in several directions, with an adjustable flow." She nodded towards the juncture of my thighs. "You've already *got* your lucky spigot. But your spacesuit doesn't have a zipper in the, um, appropriate place."

Suddenly I knew what Lilith was talking about . . . and I knew that I could get us out of here alive.

Quickly, I started to suit up for the trip outside. "You know, when I enlisted in the Fleet, I wanted to expose myself to the wonders of outer space," I said to Lilith while I hooked up the shoulder pack of my EVA life-support unit, and shrugged it into place. "But I never thought I would have to *expose myself* to outer space."

Lilith helped me put on my space helmet while I linked my environmental controls to the EVA pack's oxygen hoses and CO_2 outflow. As I switched on the air regulator, Lilith raised her voice to speak above the whirring hum of the fan motor in my EVA pack: "Right now, our shuttle has an oxygen leak, a fuel leak, a thermal leak, and a power leak." Through the faceplate of my helmet, I saw Lilith glance one more time towards the lower half of my body as she spoke: "When fate offers you nothing but leaks, your only option is to *take* one. A leak, I mean."

"What I plan to *take* are several EVA tethers," I said, not sure if she'd heard me through the visor of my space helmet. I went to the locker and unshipped several grapple-straps: D-ring tethers, designed for extra-vehicular activity. As Lilith watched, I hooked one end of each tether to the clamps on my exosuit. "Without these tethers, I'll have no way to hold on to the ship while I'm doing my business . . . because I'll have my hands full."

"Typical *male* bragging," said Lilith. "Are you sure you won't need some tweezers and a microscope?"

I ignored her remark, while I secured the wrist seals on my gloves, and I ran the final check of my environmental suit's fail-safes while I recited the safety sequence: "Lock. Blue lock. Lock-lock. Red lock. Purge lock. Set." I stepped towards the outer hatchway.

Lilith cycled the airlock; luckily, it hadn't been damaged in our collision with the microlith. I stepped into the airlock, then I turned to look back. "Ms. Virago, you're always telling me that women are just as capable as men."

"More capable," she corrected me.

"Well, then, maybe *you* should be the one to step outside and handle this particular job," I suggested.

She shook her head. "Sorry, but my bladder isn't full at the moment. And besides, this job requires a multi-directional spigot." Once again, her glance went below the waist of my spacesuit. "I never thought I would admit it, but you finally found a job that a *man* is better equipped to handle."

* * *

The outer hatch closed behind me, and I made sure I was tethered securely to several recessed hooks in the external hull before I let go of the hatchway. As I edged forward I *felt*, rather than heard, the reassuring *click* beneath my feet which told me that the soles of my boots were grabbing the shuttle's magnetized hull plates, just underneath the shuttle's thermal ablation tiles. When the Fleet's engineering wonks designed this shuttle, they picked the optimum flux density for magnetizing the hull: just enough gauss to hold my exosuit in place if I blacked out during EVA, but weak enough so that I could easily pull my boots loose and overcome the magnetic current when I *wanted* to move.

Pallas was right below me. Caught between the gravity well of my own shuttle and the larger but more distant gravitational pull of the asteroid, I felt two conflicting forms of vertigo: I was upside down, dangling from the shuttle by my feet, and feeling as if any second now I would break loose and hurtle towards Pallas . . . but at the same time I was right side up, with the immense sphere of Pallas looming overhead and ready to come crashing down on top of me.

I had to get to the far side of the hull, facing *away* from Pallas . . . so

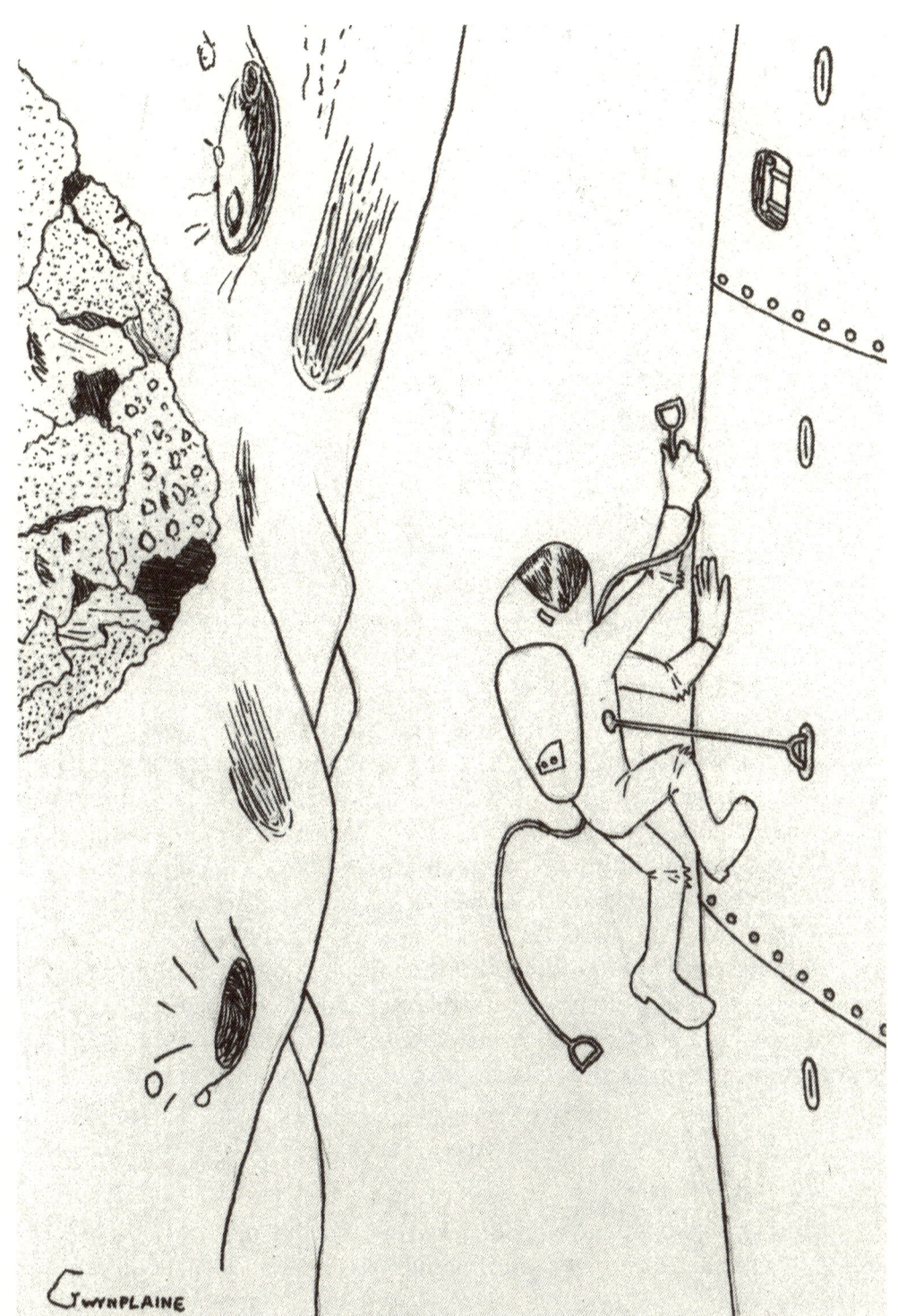

that, when I released my liquid propellant, the flow's reaction would push the shuttle *towards* the asteroid.

My spacewalk across the hull was more like a space*crawl*; in mini-gravity, any sudden burst of kinetic energy could make me attain escape velocity. I secured my forward tethers before I unhooked the D-rings behind me, then brought them overhead to become the next set of forward tethers. I kept going like this, in a human-fly act, every inch of the way. Finally, I crouched near the starboard nacelle, with the shuttle's hull between me and Pallas. Now I had a job that I would have to do *standing up*. Carefully, I straightened my knees and stood upright for action.

Far away, near the sun, I could make out the distant glow of Earth. And half in shadow, Luna. Somewhere in that shadowed disc was Tycho City. Home. If I did this job right, I might see home again.

I tried to ignore the pressure in my bladder; internal body fluids *always* feel uncomfortable in microgravity, but now my bladder felt like it was about to break loose from its moorings and float away. Well, relief was coming soon . . .

With the airtight glove on my right hand, I slid open the stow-pouch on my left sleeve. Among the small tools on tiny hooks inside the pouch was a straight-edge blade, slightly magnetized.

Easy does it, now. I would have to take a leak . . . no, *make* a leak in my own spacesuit, by cutting a hole in it so that the fluid could leak out. But I wanted to keep the *oxygen* leak as small as possible, and the *thermal* leak too. Unfortunately, any puncture in my EVA rig that was *small* enough to let a water-based fluid dribble out slowly would be *large* enough to let a fatal amount of oxygen and heat come gushing out rapidly. I would have to work damned fast . . .

With the straight-edge blade, I slit the fibers in the front of my exosuit. I cut a small hole in the outer layer of fabric, and reached inside.

Somehow, a brief speech seemed appropriate. "This will be one small leak for a man," I announced, "and one giant leak for all spacemen."

*   *   *

My liquid propellant worked just fine. So did my multi-directional spigot. By aiming the spigot in different directions, and by modifying the pressure — slowing the liquid's outflow to a dribble, shutting it off in mid-stream, then changing directions and releasing the torrent full blast — I controlled our shuttle's orbital trajectory and velocity. I coaxed the shuttle into a spiraling descent. Each time the decaying orbit brought me back to the sunlit side of Pallas, I kept a sharp lookout for the bright glint of *metal* on the asteroid's dark basalt surface. On the third flyover I spotted it, and on the fourth transit I made sure: yes, I'd found the supply drop.

I swung my spigot around and brought us into a descent, passing almost directly above the supply depot at each orbital transit. Braking was the hard part. Less than twenty meters above the surface of Pallas, I aimed my spigot and squeezed off a jet-spray of fluid straight ahead, countering the shuttle's forward momentum and slowing our velocity to near-zero. Then I turned off the spray from my makeshift garden-hose, tucked it back into my exosuit, and I crawled to the underside of the hull. Now I was in a deadly position. The shuttle's undercarriage was skimming along, almost directly above the surface of the asteroid: the two masses — Pallas and the shuttlecraft — were attracting each other, in strict accordance with the laws of gravity . . . and I was *between* them. If this didn't work, I could blame it on Isaac Newton. Or Isaac Asimov. Either way, I'd be dead.

I took out my spigot again, and let loose a controlled blast of liquid propellant to act as a retro-rocket for the final descent. I got out of the way just in time, hauling myself across the starboard nacelle as the shuttle made a cockeyed but surprisingly gentle landing on the asteroid's surface, scrunching to a halt in slow motion, in a bed of magnesium crystals. Barely fifty meters from the supply depot.

Still not done yet. In this asteroid's tiny gravity well, with its fragment of escape velocity, a sudden movement could send me flying into space. I hooked an expanding umbilical to the shuttle's hull, and clamped the other end to my exosuit. Then I stood up on the surface of Pallas.

The horizon was too close. My instincts kept screaming at me: if I took a step in any direction, I would fall off the edge of this tiny rock that was too small to be a planet. There was a thermal leak in my exosuit, where I'd slashed it open: I could see carbon dioxide vapor steaming out, and dry-ice crystals forming at the edges of the gash. I tried to ignore my vertigo, and the spreading winter-chill across my gut. Somehow, I managed to move in long microgravity strides across the cratered basalt until I reached the supply depot.

Praise be to all the solar system's saints, the distress beacon was still intact . . . and its batteries were charged. I jackplugged my helmet's comlink into the beacon's audio unit, so that I could transmit a voice-message.

I sent out a wideband SOS. After a few desperate minutes, I got an answer from the *Arthur C. Clarke*, a transport vessel in the asteroid belt's Hungarias zone. When I gave the *Clarke* my position, and told them how far I was beyond the Fleet's authorized flight vectors, it took them a few seconds to realize I wasn't joking. Then the *Clarke*'s CO took over the comlink, to give me a quick debriefing and a status update.

I would need to do some tall explaining back on Luna, when it was time for the Fleet's court of inquiry to ask why I'd taken my shuttle so far out of the ecliptic. This might go beyond a mere court of inquiry; Fleet Command could very well be convening my court-martial. But if things had gone a little differently, they'd be holding my post-mortem.

I picked up a couple of hundred-kilo oxygen cylinders from the supply depot. The pressure gauges showed they were full . . . but they weighed practically nothing on Pallas, of course. By now I felt confident enough to move freely in the asteroid's minigravity: I stood up, slung an oxygen cylinder over each shoulder, and I walked back to the airlock.

*　　*　　*

"Back so soon?" asked Lilith Virago, sounding faintly surprised. I came into the shuttle's habitat section backwards, facing away from her, because I was bending over to put down the oxygen tanks. A few drops of liquid trickled in slow motion from the gash in my exosuit. The shuttle's internal environment — Earth-normal air pressure but near-zero gravity — made the dripping liquid coalesce into tiny spheres, rolling across the deckplates like beads of quicksilver.

Lilith noticed the drip, and she saw that it was coming from the front of my spacesuit. "You've wet yourself," she observed.

I straightened up, and turned around. There was a gaping hole in the pressurized fabric, where I'd slashed open my exosuit. Lilith took a look at me . . . and then she did a double-take.

The crotch of my spacesuit was intact. The hole I'd cut into the fabric was thirty centimeters higher . . . directly above my navel. "What's that hole doing *there?*" Lilith asked.

I reached into the gash in my spacesuit, and I pulled out my spigot . . . the one I'd jerry-rigged for the emergency. When I razor-slashed the outer layer of my environmental suit, I'd been careful not to cut into the under-layer. That was the layer directly over my skin . . . and I didn't want to expose any part of my naked flesh to the frigid vacuum of space.

The original astronauts — way back in the days of the Mercury and Gemini space programs — became overheated very quickly in their bulky life-support suits, even in the coldness of space. All the post-Gemini space-suits — from the Apollo program right up to our own 21st-century rigs — have been designed to prevent that.

I showed Lilith the spigot I'd made. I had cut into the central layer of my spacesuit, and pulled loose one of the long network of narrow tubes that conveyed liquid coolant across my body. There must have been several liters of liquid in there . . . until I razored open a coolant tube, and used it as my spigot.

The tubes were made of flexible plastic, so I could aim one in any direc-tion. And by varying the pressure of my gloved fingers as I pinched the coolant tube's opening, I could vary the speed and intensity of my liquid pro-pellant as I released it. To maintain pressure in the network of tubes while I drained their contents, I kept the remaining fluid under pressure by using my other hand to squeeze progressively larger sections of my spacesuit.

Using this makeshift watering-hose, I had *sprayed* us down to the sur-face of Pallas. Now I knotted the severed ends of the slashed tube, so that I wouldn't leak any more coolant.

"And now, if you'll excuse me," I said to Lilith Virago as I strode past her towards our micrograv toilet, "I *must* attend to nature's call. My bladder has had no relief lately."

"But you . . . but I . . . but I thought . . ." Lilith was babbling incoher-ently. Her eyes shifted their attention from the leaking portion of my space-suit — at the navel — towards my crotch, and then towards my face. "Damn it," she spluttered. "You were talking about a liter of fluid in a pressurized container, and then you said that your bladder was full. So when you men-tioned a *spigot*, I thought you meant . . ."

I looked at her innocently. "Yes?"

"You know what I meant!" Lilith pointed accusingly towards my most intimate region. "Every *man's* favorite part of himself! Do I have to name the beast?"

"Evidently you do," I said.

Lilith Virago blushed three shades of maroon. "When you mentioned a multi-directional spigot," she muttered, deeply embarrassed, "I assumed that you were referring to your *penis*."

"Really?" I tried to stay deadpan. "But my penis never came up . . . as a topic of conversation, I mean. At least, *I* never mentioned it. Ms. Virago, did you seriously believe that I would use my penis like some kind of raygun, and *whiz* my way out of danger?"

Lilith Virago's face turned several colors that I'd never seen before. "Damn you, *yes!*" she hissed. "That's what I *expected* you to do! In times of crisis, every male's instinctive urge compels him to reach for . . ."

"Well, this may surprise you, Ms. Virago," I said calmly, "but — during our recent crisis — I was thinking about the liquid coolant in my spacesuit, and how it might save us. *Your* spacesuit has the same coolant system, slightly reconfigured for the contours of a female anatomy. Any *woman* trained to work in outer space could have had the same idea that *I* had . . . *if* she was thinking objectively." I tried to look gravely concerned. "But now, Ms. Virago, it seems that — when we were in danger — *you* were thinking of my penis, and regarding it as your only source of salvation." I smiled wickedly, and opened the hatchway of the micrograv latrine. "Which one of us is being phallocentric *now?*"

I went into the latrine and sealed the hatch, but the bulkhead between us wasn't thick enough to muffle the sound of Lilith's curses. Fortunately, I couldn't hear her . . . because I was laughing too hard.

I'm not looking forward to that court of inquiry back home, but I've got a hunch I'll survive it. Besides, no matter what the verdict is, I'll never have to pilot another mission alongside Lilith Virago.

While I was outside, using the transceiver of the emergency beacon on the surface of Pallas, I had a brief chat with the captain of the *Clarke*, and she told me — yes, *she* told me — that Fleet Command has posted the new duty rotations. A brand-new vessel has just come out of the Fleet's shipyards in selenocentric orbit above Luna, and Mission Specialist Lilith Virago will be part of its first crew.

The Fleet is sending Lilith on the first manned mission to Pluto. *Manned* is the appropriate word: the ship will be crewed by twenty-seven Fleet officers, and all of the chosen personnel — except for Lilith Virago — are *male*. Big strapping spacemen who will feel a hankering for some female companionship on those cold lonely Pluto-side nights. Maybe Lilith will keep her shipmates entertained with a few snappy lectures about how they should get in touch with their inner female spirituality. Could be a very interesting mission. I'm sure glad I won't be along on that particular ride, though.

And Lilith Virago will be going to Pluto aboard that brand-new pride of the Fleet: the spaceship *Isaac Asimov*.

I wrote 'The Man Who Split in Twain' in late 1985. Halley's Comet was due back for a visit to Earth; I wanted to write a story about the comet's return, and to have it appear in print *at the same time* that Halley's Comet returned. George Scithers was editing *Amazing Stories* at the time. He assured me that, if I could write an appropriate story speedily enough, it would appear in his magazine at the appropriate date. Sure enough, 'The Man Who Split in Twain' was published in the May 1986 *Amazing* . . . which, thanks to the time warp of magazine cover-dating, went on sale in <u>February</u> 1986, when Halley's Comet was on everybody's lips (so to speak). I even got my name listed on the cover of that issue.

I assume that you already know the link between Halley's Comet and Mark Twain. (If not, it's mentioned in this story.) Mark Twain is one of my favourite authors. He was also a deeply troubled man, plagued with many obsessions. One of his obsessions was the dual nature of the human soul. In Mark Twain's diary entry for the night of 7 January 1897 — written while he lived at 23 Tedworth Square, London — he described an occasion four nights earlier in which he encountered his own *Doppelgänger*. On many occasions during his lifetime — even on his deathbed — Twain referred to himself as both a Jekyll and a Hyde. This grim fact — and his link to Halley's Comet — inspired me to write 'The Man Who Split in Twain'.

Because this story is set in London, I've written most of it in a modern British idiom . . . but I've rendered Mark Twain's dialogue in a nineteenth-century American idiom. This explains why, for instance, the word 'whisky' is spelt two different ways. However, the story was meant for American readers, so I've used a few Yank terms, such as 'floor lamp' instead of the British 'standard lamp'.

A few words about that house in Tedworth Square. In 'The Man Who Split in Twain', I employed the unusual device — unusual for *me*, at least — of casting myself as my own story's fictional narrator. For purposes of this story, I claimed to live in Mark Twain's former residence at 23, Tedworth Square. This is, of course, a real address in S.W.3, London. When I wrote 'The Man Who Split in Twain', that house was occupied by a family named Johnstone, who very kindly indulged my researches. Since I was claiming to live there, I was concerned that mail addressed to me might arrive in the Johnstones' letter-slot. Therefore, I persuaded George to let me attach a postscript (not reprinted here) at the end of my story, in which I divulged my real address and asked readers to direct their correspondence accordingly.

In 1986, when this story was originally published, I was living at Number 6, Albemarle Way, in the Clerkenwell district of east London, directly above a cut-sandwich shop. I reluctantly gave up this address because Her Majesty's Post Office kept mistakenly routing my mail to Number 6, Albemarle <u>Street</u>, which is the address of the Marlborough Art Gallery. The fact that a sub-district post office is situated directly across the street from the Marlborough Art Gallery did not seem to help matters much.

'The Man Who Split in Twain' is now a period piece, not only because it takes place during the 1986 return of Halley's Comet, but for other reasons as well. The Greater London Council, which I mention in this story, was alive and unwell in 1986 but has now (thankfully) gone the way of the dinosaur.

In this story, I make the curious claim that Mark Twain once wrote an essay about a 'previous occupant' of my name. I admit that my middle name, Gwynplaine, is an affectation. Although it sounds Welsh, the name 'Gwynplaine' was invented by Victor Hugo: his novel **The Man Who Laughs** features a character with that name, and I took the name because I identified with Hugo's fictional hero. In 1869, shortly after Victor Hugo's novel was published, Mark Twain wrote a satirical essay for the Buffalo *Express* in which he borrowed the name 'Gwynplaine' and applied it to a protagonist who was apparently based on President Andrew Johnson. Thus my link to Mark Twain.

This story is not entirely fictional: I actually did live above some punk-rockers once. In 1982, my wife Lenore and I lived in a walk-up at 157 Suffolk Street, New York City. Our neighbours in the flat directly beneath were Wendy O. Williams (the lead singer of the Plasmatics) and one of her back-up musicians. (The comic-book artist Jack Kirby, creator of Captain America and other immortals, had lived in that same building many years earlier.) At weekends, Ms. Williams and I would do our laundries in the nearby launderette. Although she wore garish outfits and a stiffly-moussed mohawk onstage, in civilian life she dressed modestly in torn jeans and kept her blond mohawk tied down in a kerchief. While our undies shared a dryer, Wendy Williams would tell me her philosophy of life. She seemed obsessed with suicide, and I was not surprised several years later — after we were no longer neighbours — when she did indeed kill herself.

On that morbid note, I present 'The Man Who Split in Twain'.

THE MAN WHO SPLIT IN TWAIN

Originally published in *Amazing Stories*, May 1986.

I was advised that the house at Number 23, Tedworth Square, S.W.3, is haunted. This did not surprise me, as it is widely known that the number of ghosts desiring London accommodations far exceeds the number of houses available, and many landlords and London estate agents maintain long waiting-lists for all the ghosts, ghouls, assorted hobgoblins, and miscellaneous poltergeists who wish to abandon their crypts and castles in the provinces and seek more profitable haunting-grounds within London.

I was aware of 23 Tedworth Square's peculiar history: the three-storey building near Chelsea Embankment had once been Mark Twain's private home. When he and his family lived there — during the period from October 1896 until Queen Victoria's Diamond Jubilee in July of the following year — the Clemenses were the sole occupants. Nowadays the house is divided into separate flats so that several groups of total strangers, who might otherwise have been forced to reside in different buildings and never make one another's acquaintance, can now live together under one roof and despise one another.

I obtained lodgings at Number Twenty-Three, in the second-storey back, in January of 1985. The estate agent quoted a price so astronomically immense that I knew him instantly for a blood-descendant of Blackbeard the Pirate, and he committed further crimes against humanity by demanding three months' rent in advance: payable in the form of cash, cheque, or first-born child. I wrote the highwayman a cheque: he pocketed it, and gave me a look which implied he would return the next day with a crowbar to extract the gold in my teeth.

In the next several months I saw no evidence that the building was infested with ghosts or other supernatural claptrap, except that one of my downstairs neighbours — Mrs Buggins, in the ground-floor front — bore a definite resemblance to a banshee. The only other apparitions worth mentioning were three punk-rock musicians with polka-dot mohawks, who called themselves Snoggo and the Wankers, and who rented rooms directly beneath mine shortly after

I moved in. At first I was afraid that their musical rehearsals would keep me awake all night; fortunately, it appears that punk-rock musicians never rehearse.

I confess that I derived a certain pleasure from living in the same rooms once occupied by Mark Twain, and my interest in the man and his work — rather keen to begin with — grew steadily stronger. Gradually one corner of my den was given over to Mark Twain artefacts: I obtained several volumes of his novels and a bound collection of his magazine stories and essays. After long negotiation with several antiques dealers and other extortionists, I became the proud owner of three antique photographs of Mark Twain (one of them autographed); a green armchair that had once belonged to Mark Twain, from his country home in Guildford, Surrey; an Edison's Magniscope film of *Mark Twain at Stormfield*; an empty balsa-wood box, the label of which assured me that it had once contained Mark Twain Brand Nickel Cigars ("Known to Everyone, Liked by All, Genuine Sumatra Wrapper"); a Mark Twain cigarette-card from a packet of Mogul Cigarette Papers ("Let All Your Troubles End in Smoke!"); and a 1906 four-colour broadsheet advertisement recovered from the wall of an ancient Connecticut barn, sporting Mark Twain's scowling visage and advising me that Mr Twain endorsed the firm of Hilliar & Mallory ("Plumbers, Steamfitters and Gas, Dealers in Stoves, Ranges, Furnaces, and Lead Pipe to the Trade"). These items were all lovingly displayed in a corner of my den, to the vast amusement of my house-guests and the vaster depletion of my bank balance. The empty Mark Twain cigar-box I replenished with a fiver's worth of stogies from a tobacconist's shop in the King's Road, and I evicted a colony of blackbeetles from the upholstery of the armchair. I read the Mark Twain books upon occasion, and went on with what passes for my life.

In November of 1985, Halley's Comet returned. At November's beginning a flicker-dim point of light appeared in the evening sky, midway between Aldebaran and the Pleiades. It drew gradually closer to Earth, elbowing its way past intervening constellations in its haste to keep its appointment with the solar system. Each successive night, the flickering grew brighter as the wanderer returned from outer space.

On Earth, a wide range of reactions were aroused by the comet's approach. The astronomers, for the most part — those dedicated tireless individuals who maintain a constant vigil of the stars, in search of new and different reasons to obtain research grants — the astronomers got off their azimuths, squinted into their telescopes, saw Halley's approach, and harrumphed: "What, a rerun?

Seen it before. Already know how it ends. What else is on?" They changed channels and left Halley's alone. But the comet kept hurtling Earthwards. Seventy-three new religions sprang into existence in California, India, and East Grinstead: each of them prophesying the end of the world, and all of them soliciting funds so as not to be caught without bus-fare to Heaven on Judgment Day. None of this occupied a great deal of my thoughts, as I was single-mindedly slaving away at my life's work of grinding out manuscripts for magazine articles, short stories, and novels . . . all of which I write in order to help editors find a home for their vastly swollen stockpiles of rejection slips. By the end of January, I had papered the walls of two rooms and the foyer with rejection slips, and was preparing for a similar assault on the den.

On the night of 8 February, 1986, Halley's Comet attained its closest position to the Sun. I was not home that evening, having made one of my frequent nocturnal forays to the local pub, the Wicker Man, in order to conduct further research on the effect of alcohol upon the human nervous system. Towards midnight, however, I was on my way home. As I passed Albert Bridge, I received an excellent view of the approaching comet, a few degrees to the east of Capricorn. *What an incredible sight*, I realised. *To think that all Mankind everywhere are pausing just now, in the midst of their warfare and madness and hate, to look up at the sky for one night filled with wonder and awe, to see the comet return, and all Humanity bears witness to the incredible marvels of our boundless and unlimited universe. There must be some way I can make a buck out of this. Maybe if I sell advertising space on the comet? No, too complicated. Comet insurance? Perhaps. Maybe a book deal with . . .*

I was still wading knee-deep in thoughts, then, when I reached Tedworth Square, climbed the stairs to my second-floor flat, and went in. My conscious mind had gone off on bank-holiday elsewhere as my subconscious mind flung its coat in the general direction of the floor, inspected the latest batch of incoming rejection slips (*"Dear Sir: We cannot use the stack of paper you sent us. Somebody typed on it"*), went into the den, fixed itself a drink, switched on the late-late movie on Anglia TV (*Carry On Caligula*, starring Bob Monkhouse and Cicely Courtneidge), and deposited itself in a chair. Then and only then, as I succumbed to the pleasant effects of gin and bitters ravaging my bloodstream and the distant sound of my liver whimpering for mercy, I suddenly became aware of the aroma of cigar smoke.

I turned. Sitting there in his own armchair, filching yet another stogie from my cigar-box while the butt-ends of two others smouldered nearby, and helping himself to my personal whisky, sat Mister Mark Twain.

Not the *ghost* of Mark Twain, I was certain, nor an actor in crepe whiskers and collodion-putty. An actor would have passed up my cigars in favour of a raid on my refrigerator, and ghosts are not commonly known to fancy Scotch whisky. (The form of spirits preferred in the spirit-world, I am told, is Boo-jolais.) No, the man in the armchair was the genuine article, right enough: Mark Twain himself.

"Delighted to meet you," I said to my guest, switching off the television just as Bob Monkhouse was disguising himself as Cicely Courtneidge. "Although *seeing* you, Mister Twain, comes as rather a surprise. I had thought you were dead."

"I believe," said Mark Twain, as he took another puff on the cigar, "that the precise wording of my statement to the London correspondent of the New York *Journal* went as follows: *'The report of my death was an exaggeration.'* Yes, I died, and was offered lodge membership in Heaven if I would give up cigars and profanity. That was intolerable to me, so I took my business to their competitors — in the *Other* Place — but I was told by the Purgatory boys that I could only be let into Hell on a trial basis, as they had their reputation to think of. Well, sir, Hell was pleasant enough — I was reunited with many of my old friends down there — until I organized a labor strike among Brother Lucifer's furnace-stokers — Brimstone Local 482 — and that got me into trouble. Murderers and horse-thieves are welcome in Hell, but union organizers are not to be tolerated. So here I am."

"I'm surprised," I admitted, "to see you here in London, though. Surely you would be more at home in Missouri, or at your home in Connecticut . . ."

"Both places be thundered," snorted Mark Twain. He produced a calabash pipe from the pocket of his suit and began vivisecting my cigars, tamping their tobacco into the bowl of his pipe. "This house in Tedworth Square was always my favorite home: too many corpses and assorted unpleasantries in all the other places. And I have long been fond of England: I've always said it's a pity to waste England on the English. But I couldn't face going back to my *other* English home, the one in Surrey: I was there, living in Guilford, when my darling Susy died. Fact, London is the only place I ever lived where no memories haunt me, and now I come back to my old home and find you've got my room all laid out with my chair and my books and cigars, so how could I refuse the invitation?

Well, Jesus H. Christ, man! I appreciate a considerate host, sir, as they are generally the kind most easily taken advantage of."

"I find your timing is remarkable," I said to Mark Twain. "You've come back only just in time to see Halley's Comet."

"Why should *that* matter?" said the great man abruptly, which I thought very strange. For it is well known that, on the night Mark Twain was born, in 1835, Halley's Comet was in the sky above Earth, and he often predicted that he would die when the comet returned in 1910 . . . which in fact was what actually happened. Why did he show no great concern, therefore, towards Halley's Comet *now?*

"I have nothing against Halley's Comet," said Twain, lighting his calabash southpaw-fashion. "It occurs to me that any ball of ice which passes Earth, takes one look at the human race, and has the sense to stay away for another seventy-six years is extremely commendable."

"The comet is only partially visible from my window," I said. "The dome of Chelsea Hospital, just south of here, is in the way. However, if you'd care to accompany me into the street . . ."

"I have no particular desire to see the comet," said Samuel Langhorne Clemens. "I intend to sit here and smoke all your cigars, and drink all of your whiskey, and in general ignore all my doctor's instructions. As soon as you've run out of tobacco and liquor — then at that point, sir, your company will become intolerable to me."

I had the impression that Mark Twain had said something extremely *wrong*, but I could not think precisely what it was. The thought struck me that Twain's behaviour was unaccountably rude, but I reminded myself that I was in the presence of a man who had insulted some of the greatest minds of the past two centuries, so I accepted the honour. "I daresay it's a privilege of sorts," I told Mark Twain, "to be insulted by you. I know that you insulted Lewis Carroll and Winston Churchill when you met them, and when you were introduced to Rudyard Kipling — thereby disproving his motto 'Never the Twain shall meet' — you also insulted *him*. I should be honoured to have something in common with such eminent targets."

Mark Twain stiffened as I spoke, and I thought that he betrayed some unease. "You seem to know a good deal about me, Mister . . . ?"

"MacIntyre is the alias I'm currently using," I said. "At least, until my creditors catch up with it. At present I am named F. Gwynplaine MacIntyre."

"You choose a curious name to inhabit," Mark Twain puffed again at his pipe. "I wrote an essay on one of its previous occupants, back in 1869."

"I have read it."

"Have you?" Mark Twain suddenly bounded out of his chair and loped over to the bookcase, stooping slightly to examine the titles on my shelf. "You appear to have quite a number of my books here."

"I have read," I informed him, "not counting the manuscript fragments which do not survive, everything you ever wrote."

"That's impossible, sir."

"Not at all," I told Samuel Clemens. "I've read the newspaper dispatches you wrote under other names, before you took the pseudonym Mark Twain. Your *first* pen-name, I think, was . . ." I had to look up the precise spelling as I spoke, *"W. Epaminondas Adrastus Blab.* For some reason, that pen-name never caught on with the public. Next, you became *Thomas Jefferson Snodgrass,* and . . ."

Now this is really quite odd. As I said the name *"Thomas"*, Mark Twain turned quite suddenly pale. If it is possible for a man who has been dead for three-quarters of a century to *shudder,* Mark Twain shuddered. But he regained his composure quickly enough, and interrupted me.

"I was never fond of that name," said Samuel Langhorne Clemens. "I wrote as Thom-. . . er, as Jefferson Snodgrass *once,* but gave it up. My next pen-name was Quintus Curtius Snodgrass. And after *that,* sir, I called myself Mark Twain, after my Mississippi river-pilot days. 'Mark Twain', of course, was the leadsman's call when the riverboat struck two fathoms' depth."

"There were *two* Mark Twains, were there not?" I asked.

Clemens stiffened again, but this time I was not surprised. Like many Mark Twainophiles (*Twainophiliacs? Twainomaniacs? never mind!*) I knew that there was *another* Mississippi river pilot who had called himself Mark Twain. He was Captain Isaiah B. Sellers, and in the 1850s he wrote for the New Orleans *Picayune* under the by-line "Mark Twain". Samuel Clemens was aware of this, having served under Captain Sellers aboard — I looked it up — the riverboat *William H. Morrison* on its St. Louis-New Orleans run, in July of 1857. Isaiah Sellers had been Mark Twain ten years before Sam Clemens ever got his hands on the monicker . . . and it was widely known, when Clemens first began to find success as "Mark Twain" a few years later, that he had stolen another man's pen-name. Samuel Clemens was uncomfortable about this for the rest of his life. I saw that I had made an indiscretion in confronting the dead man with the fact of his name-theft, so I hastened to placate him: "Even though you were not the *first* Mark Twain," I said quickly, reaching for the whisky bottle and refilling Clemens's glass, "you were definitely the more talented of the two. No one remembers Isaiah Sellers these days."

I was surprised when, as I said this, Clemens relaxed completely. I thought that there was even some semblance of a *smile* beneath his white moustache. "I misunderstood," he nodded, accepting the drink. "When you spoke of two Twains, you meant myself and *Sellers*."

"Of course. Who *else* could I have meant?"

"You mentioned the comet . . . ," said Mark Twain, bringing this thought out of nowhere, and I am not so unobservant that I fail to notice when a subject is pulled out from under me. Samuel Clemens had preferred not to speak of Halley's Comet before, yet now when I raised the subject of duplicate Twains he seized the comet eagerly enough as the more desirable topic of discussion. Something was decidedly wrong here, for no novelist ever born — not Mark Twain, nor any other — ever wants to shift the subject of conversation *away from himself*. Novelists, every single last one of them, are a thoroughly conceited and egotistical lot . . . with the sterling exception, of course, of myself. (I am not the least bit conceited, although I have every right to be.) As I thought of this, I went over to the mirror to admire my . . .

"EEEP!" I eeped eebruptly.

"Something wrong?" Mark Twain asked me, hoisting his drink.

"Glub," I replied, goggling at what I saw in the mirror. "Jumping Kallikaks!"

"Speak up, boy!" said Mark Twain. "Don't talk nonsense. That job's reserved for editors and Congressmen."

I was staring at the mirror, the reflection in the glass. My face was there, devilishly handsome as always. And behind me I saw the reflection of the other in the room. *But it wasn't Mark Twain.*

In the surface of the glass I saw the mirror-image chair, and in the mirror-chair sat Mark Twain's mirror-self. But the thing in the looking-glass chair was inhuman. I saw the reflection of a hideous dwarf, a hunchbacked thing shaped like a *caricature* of Mark Twain . . . for Twain's features, mashed and perverted, could still be picked out in the newcomer's face. It was a wizened homunculus, barely two feet tall, its flesh encrusted with some sort of green fungoid growth, and it was sitting in Mark Twain's armchair, calmly drinking my whisky and smoking a cigar — as real as life, and quite as unnatural.

I turned away from the mirror, and looked back at the chair. It was full of Mark Twain again, or something shaped exactly like him. The cigar-smoking dwarf had vanished, and the genuine pipe-smoking Mark Twain was there, ignoring me and devoting his full attention to my whisky.

I looked back at the mirror, and saw the ghastly reflection again, where Mark Twain should have been. The shape in the mirror was a dwarf with a cigar.

The most frightening thing about the image in the looking-glass was that it looked extremely *familiar*. I felt certain that I had encountered this creature somewhere before. But how could I have seen such a hideous thing, and not *remember* it? There had to be some other . . .

Then I knew where it had come from.

My coat was on the floor where I had hung it. I picked it up now, and tried to appear casual. "I'm going out for a bit," I told the thing in the armchair. "After tonight, Halley's Comet won't come back again until . . . hmm, let's see, carry the seven . . . until 2061, give or take the odd fortnight. I ought to see it *tonight*, while I'm still healthy enough. In 2061, I might not be feeling so chipper."

"Please yourself," said the thing that pretended to be Mark Twain, without looking up. It had finished most of the scotch, and was turning its attention to my gin.

I edged towards the bookshelf, put my coat on with a casual flourish that was meant to look debonair, and I suavely knocked several books to the floor. "Sorry," I stammered, hastily picking up the books. *Is this the proper one? Right; got it.* I hid the book in my coat, and returned the other volumes to the shelf. "I am just going outside and may be gone for some time," I said, scurrying towards the door.

"No hurry," grunted the counterfeit Mark Twain. As I left, the creature struck another lucifer-match and began reading my mail.

I got the hell out of there. "Evening, squire," said a trio of figures sporting polka-dot mohawks and cummerbunds, as they passed me on the stairs. They were carrying two violins and a 'cello: Snoggo and the Wankers had been unable to obtain any punk-rock concert bookings of late, and the Labour Exchange had forced them to accept temporary employment — at far lower wages and fewer job benefits — as musicians with the London Symphony Orchestra. I tripped over Snoggo's 'cello-case, careened off the stair-posts, and then I was downstairs and into the street.

Halley's Comet was still overhead, towards the southern horizon. By its light, and by the spasmodic flicker of a malfunctioning street-lamp that had not been repaired since 1917 (thank you, Greater London Council), I took out the book I had concealed in my coat, and I started to read . . .

It was a collection of Mark Twain's essays and short stories; I flipped about through the pages until I found what I was looking for: a science-fiction story titled "The Facts Concerning the Recent Carnival of Crime in Connecticut". This peculiar tale of Mark Twain's had originally been published — it said here — in the June 1876 number of the *Atlantic* magazine; I have read it often, always annoyed that the modern-day editors of *Atlantic* do not buy science-fiction stories as readily as their more enlightened nineteenth-century counterparts did. But now, when I thought of the thing that lurked in my room in Tedworth Square, it occurred to me that "Carnival of Crime" might not be fiction after all . . .

I started reading Mark Twain's science-fiction yarn again. It was written in the first person, and from various clues within the text it was evident that the narrator of this tale was Samuel Langhorne Clemens himself.

Only a supreme egomaniac, I thought while I turned the pages, *would write a story with* himself *as the narrator.*

I kept reading. In the story, Samuel Clemens was alone in his room, when suddenly

> . . . *the door opened, and a shriveled, shabby dwarf entered. He was not more than two feet high. Every feature and inch of him was a trifle out of shape, a deformity. There was a cunning in the face and the sharp little eyes, an alertness and malice. And yet, this vile bit of human rubbish seemed to bear a resemblance to* me! *He was a far-fetched suggestion of a burlesque upon me, a caricature of me in miniature. He was covered all over with a fuzzy greenish mould, and the sight of it was nauseating . . .*

I read more rapidly, skipped the story's embellishments, and reread crucial passages.

The dwarf in the story sat down in the narrator's chair and proceeded to accuse its host (Samuel Clemens himself) of a series of sins and indiscretions. Some of the crimes of which Clemens is accused by the dwarf are not immoral acts, but merely improper *thoughts*. Every single accusation is true, but Clemens cannot imagine how the intruder could have witnessed his privatemost acts and audited his very thoughts. Then Clemens confronts his accuser:

"I think you are Satan himself," I replied.
"I am not," said the devilish pygmy.
"Then who can you be?"
"I am your Conscience!"

And then I saw the answer. And I knew what sort of creature had invaded my rooms.

Halley's Comet was streaking towards Battersea Rise as I ran back upstairs to my flat and confronted the thing in the armchair.

"I know who you are," I said, approaching my visitor.

"Of course you do," remarked the thing that had copied Mark Twain's shape. "Hail Columbia, man! I'm Sam Clemens."

"That's a lie," I said, taking out a pen and some paper. "There are three elements in Mark Twain's writings that have always mystified me. The first is his fixation with *twins*. I can think of at least a dozen sets of twins in the stories of Mark Twain. There are John Canty's twin daughters in *The Prince and the Pauper*, the Lathers twins in Twain's novella *The American Claimant*, the Italian twins in *Pudd'nhead Wilson*, the *two* sets of twins in *The Gilded Age*, the twins in *Was it Heaven? or Hell?*, the twins in . . ."

"That's enough twins for the moment," said the ersatz Mark Twain. "I'm beginning to see double."

"The *second* curious element in Mark Twain's work," I went on, "is his fixation with dual personalities, of Good and Evil as counter-versions of the same man." I took a volume from the shelf: it was Robert Louis Stevenson's 1886 novel *The Strange Case of Dr Jekyll and Mr Hyde*. "This book," I remarked to my visitor, "affected Samuel Clemens more profoundly than any other work he had ever read. Purely on the basis of *Jekyll and Hyde*, Clemens sought an introduction to Robert Louis Stevenson. They are known to have spent several hours together one afternoon in New York City, discussing dual personalities. In one of his own notebooks, Mark Twain wrote: *'Every man is a moon, and has a dark side which he never shows to anybody.'* And it is a matter of historical record that, *on his deathbed, Mark Twain raved about Jekyll and Hyde, and insisted that both of their personalities were present in himself.*"

In the stillness of the room, my caller shifted in his chair. "Pray go on," said the simulation of Clemens. "This has become most interesting."

Did his features change slightly, as he spoke? In the dim light, it was difficult to tell.

"The word 'twain', of course, means *double*," I said, speaking quickly, before I might run out of nerve. "This leads to the *third* theme within Mark Twain's work: the *Doppelgänger*. Several of Twain's novels contain two men, or two boys, who are not brothers but who are of identical appearance. In each case, invariably, one of the two steals the other's identity, thus forcing the second to take the identity of the first, or to assume an alias. Shall I set down for you a list of the Doppelgängers populating the works of Mark Twain?"

I drew up a list, and gave this to the stranger. "See if you can discover the common element," I challenged him.

This was the list:

In each of these stories by Mark Twain . . .	. . . the character who is named . . .	. . . trades identities with his own *Doppelgänger*, who is named:
The Prince and the Pauper	Edward Tudor	**THOMAS** Canty
The Adventures of Huckleberry Finn	Huckleberry Finn	**THOMAS** ("Tom") Sawyer
Pudd'nhead Wilson	Valet de Chambre	**THOMAS** à Becket Driscoll
Which Was the Dream?	Jeff Sedgewick	**THOMAS** X.

"You will note," I observed to the visitor, "that there is, as Mark Twain might have put it, a definite surplusage of Thomases. For some reason, Mark Twain created a whole procession of characters whose greatest pleasure is to switch lives with their own physical doubles, all of whom were conveniently named *Thomas*."

The thing in the armchair regarded me solemnly. Without moving, it *shifted*. It began to look less like Mark Twain, and more like . . . *another*. "Remarkable," said the mysterious stranger. "I do believe that *you have figured out the secret*."

"I had one other clue," I told my visitor, "and it came from the Bible. Mark Twain was an atheist; he chose to disbelieve the Scriptures, but he read them frequently and was obsessed with them. I have read the Bible myself — I except to find a loophole in it *one* of these days — and I know that it says, in the Gospel of Saint John, where Mark Twain has surely seen it, that *the name 'Thomas' means 'twin'*."

"I congratulate you," said the changing visitor. "You are not so stupid as you look."

"You are not any fragment of Clemens," I said to the stranger. "I know you, and your name means 'double twin'. You are Thomas Twain, the *Doppelgänger* of Samuel Clemens, the counter-version of himself that pursued Mark Twain all his life, that populated his nightmares, that hounded him to his deathbed."

The thing in the armchair, having no further use for its face, removed it. Then it took off its arms and legs and pocketed them carefully, forming cavities within itself to engulf them. *"Much* better," it sighed, assuming quite another shape entirely. The creature seemed, at this point, to be composed less of physical matter than of fluctuating light — dimming and brightening just the same way as other beings might breathe in and out. It left the armchair, and hovered near my bookshelf. *"Now, then,"* the pulsating brightness went on, *"since you know this much, you very likely can guess all the rest."*

"You gave yourself away," I told the visitor. "You said something which struck me as wrong, but I couldn't quite place what it was at the time. Now I remember: Samuel Clemens was fascinated by Halley's Comet, and by comets in general, but during his lifetime no one knew much about comets' physical nature. Most scientists of Mark Twain's time believed that comets were composed of flaming gas. Yet during our conversation this evening you referred to Halley's Comet, quite accurately, as a ball of *ice*."

For a time neither one of us spoke. I heard the ticking of my clock in a corner of the room . . . and through the window, far away across the midnight London, to the east, in the Pimlico streets behind Victoria Station, I could hear the faint distant sounds of Borstal youth gangs gently breaking one another's skulls. At last, having finished its silence, my visitor spoke:

"I arrived on the comet," the flicker-thing said. *"My people are the wanderers, who belong to no star-system, yet pass amongst them all . . ."*

"The comets. Of course." I nodded, and reached for my pipe. "D'you mean to say you use comets for spaceships?"

"No. Our vessels the comets are more like . . ." — it seemed to grope about for the proper word — *". . . the comets are like Phoenix eggs. They nurture us in our voyage through the interstellar space. They birth us. We awaken when our vessels carry us close to some star, and the warmth rouses us. Afterwards, when the comet's flight has left the nearest star behind us, we sleep . . . until rebirth and reawakening, when our comet brings us near another star."*

I had recently read several papers in scientific journals, presenting evidence that comets may contain organic matter. I had never suspected, when I read of it, that the organic matter in question might one evening enter my flat and prop its feet on my furniture, and help itself to my whisky and cigars. To the comet-visitor I said: "Explain, if you please, your relationship to Mark Twain."

"I passed this planet," said the wanderer, *"in 1835, by your calendar's reckoning, though I knew nothing of clocks nor calendars at the time. I decided that it would be fun to leave Star-Mother temporarily, and . . ."*

"Star-Mother being Halley's Comet?"

"Yes. I knew that there would be plenty of time for me to explore, because Star-Mother would remain within reach of your world for several days. And so I left Star-Mother's vessel, and journeyed towards Earth . . ."

I was about to interrupt again, and ask this creature *how* it had made its passage from Halley's Comet planetwards. Then I recalled having read that some organic compounds — amino acids, protein chains, and the like — often travel through space, aboard the solar wind. I said nothing, and my visitor continued:

"I reached Earth, although at the time I did not know this planet's name. And I was surprised to discover . . ." — again, the visitor paused, as if searching for a word — *". . . to find* presences, *much like myself, but trapped within curious vessels."*

"Entities, do you mean? Intelligences?" I asked. "Human minds in living bodies?"

"Precisely! I came among them. I listened to one presence here, touched another thought somewhere else. I passed among the corridors of minds until . . . now this is the peculiar part . . . I sensed a presence that was forming thoughts about ME!"

"Was this, by chance," I asked the star-guest, "in Missouri?"

"So you name the region, yes. I found myself drawn towards one particular beacon of consciousness, and as I drew closer I discovered that it was actually two *entities — one fully sentient, the other aware and yet somehow also dormant — and both presences dwelt in one vessel. For some reason, the primary entity seemed to regard the dormant second mind within itself as being somehow . . . interchangeable with my own vessel the comet."*

"I can explain that," I offered. "Mark Twain's mother believed in astrology, and drew connections between her children and their birth-stars. She named her eldest son Orion Clemens, simply because Orion was the brightest constellation in the sky on the night of his birth."

I went to the bookcase, consulted a volume, and searched until I found the proper passage. "Yes, here it is! Halley's Comet attained perihelion on the sixteenth of November, 1835; Samuel Clemens was born a few days later. It says here — I'll paraphrase it — that Jane Lampton Clemens, happening to look up shortly before her son Samuel's birth, saw Halley's Comet pass overhead, and at the same time she felt her young *steerage passenger* stirring within her. Obviously, having named one son for a constellation, she would not hesitate — given the circumstances — to draw connections between another son and Halley's Comet. What happened next?"

"*I drew closer to this double entity,*" said my visitor, "*drawn towards it partly by my will, and partly borne on the current of thoughts. For thoughts travel in currents, you see; some attracting other minds, and some repelling them. The thought-self before me was beckoning, and I felt it welcome me, saying: 'You and the comet, together, have come.'*"

"Understandable," I nodded. "Jane Clemens, feeling the movements of her unborn son Samuel, must have been directing her thoughts towards him. Or did you sense that she was addressing *you?*" I asked my guest.

"*Myself, yes, and the dormant other,*" said the wanderer. "*I began to grow frightened. I tried to leave, to return to the comet. But by now the current of thought-stream drawing me towards this wakening presence was so strong that I could no longer fight against it. I was trying to find my vessel, the comet Star-Mother, but the stronger entity in my presence kept insisting that it held the comet, something very like the comet, here within its own body. It was all so confusing . . .*"

"No doubt, since Jane Clemens felt that her son personified the comet. *Then* what?"

"*And then the second mind-presence, the dormant one, became suddenly awake all at once. It reached out for every possible sensation, clutching hold of every stimulus its mind could touch . . .*"

"An unusual, but accurate description," I said, "of the birth-trauma."

"*I was consumed, drawn into the awakening entity, and I was too exhausted and confused to escape. I felt myself drawn in two different directions: by the Earthbound mind that had engulfed me, and by Star-Mother, my comet. But all this time the mind that held me grew stronger, while my comet Star-Mother, far off now, grew ever more distant away . . .*"

". . . and your star-vessel did not return," I said, lighting my pipe, "until 1910, at the time of Mark Twain's death." I consulted the book again.

"Halley's Comet appeared that year in the constellation Orion; it attained zenith on 19 April, and Mark Twain died at sunset two days later. Is that when you returned to the stars?"

"It was," said my guest. "Having been trapped, for seventy-five years' interim, in the body and mind of Samuel Langhorne Clemens. Only his death could release me."

I felt the need for a drink. "I only hope," I remarked to my visitor, "that the von Däniken brigade never hears about this. They'll claim that Mark Twain's novels were written by extraterrestrials . . ."

"I never wrote a word of Mark Twain's work," said the star-born. "His genius was his own. But I brought him his madness."

"Please explain."

"Separated from Star-Mother, I could not survive without a vessel to inhabit. I was forced to adapt Samuel Clemens's mind so that it could sustain me. Gradually, as Clemens grew older, he became more aware of my presence within him, and he welcomed this. He named me Thomas, or Tom, for the Biblical twin . . . and he offered me haven within his mind."

"Two questions, though," I asked the visitor. "Firstly: why did you come back to Earth tonight, after so many years? And secondly: why, when I first met you, did you pretend to be Mark Twain?"

"I can tell you that," said a voice in the corner. I looked, and there in his armchair sat Mark Twain himself. The mane of hair, the moustache-whiskers, were unmistakable. The Great Curmudgeon had returned.

"There you are, Tom, you body-thieving bucketsnipe," said Mark Twain to the pinpoint of light. "Come on out here, where a man can get a look of you."

"I am here," said the comet-born wanderer. The pinpoint of light changed again, shifted into a material form. And now it was the misshapen dwarf that I had seen in the mirror, the moss-covered caricature of Samuel Clemens, from his story "The Carnival of Crime": the form in which Mark Twain perceived his inner self.

"There are all kinds of prisons," said Mark Twain to his dark twin. "So you were trapped in my mind, Tom? I was trapped in the worst prison ever devised. Shall I tell you about it?"

"I believe," I said quickly, "that this is hardly the time . . ."

"Keep quiet, you!" Mark Twain glared at me, while filching one of my ash-trays. His eyes, I observed, were of an unusual colour: green and grey in equal quantities. "I didn't come here to help you make a fool of yourself," Mark Twain told me. "I believe that you can manage that job without my assistance. I've been listening to your blatherments: you know a bit about Mark Twain, but you don't know two cents' worth of Sam Clemens. Sit down and listen, and maybe you'll learn something. And pass me those cigars."

I passed him the cigar-box, and sat down.

Mark Twain be-stogied himself, then reached into his pocket and extracted a flaming lump of coal. He lit the cigar with this, and took a tentative puff.

"Not the Dunhill Havanas I always favored," he declared. "But a decent cheroot nonetheless. Better, at any rate, than the Missouri toby-weeds my father always smoked. Now, then: I've come a long way to be here tonight." He indicated the burning-hot coal in his hand. "At my current address they pave the street with these things, and call 'em Purgatory bed-warmers." He flung the coal into my fireplace and puffed the cigar.

"I was remarking on my imprisonment," said Mark Twain to myself and the star-twin. "I was condemned, without jury or trial, to serve a sentence of seventy-five years in the body and life of Samuel Clemens. My earliest memory is this: when I was three years old, back in Missouri, my mother showed me the corpse of my older sister Margaret, in her coffin. So my life, for all practical purposes, begins at Margaret's death. When I was six, in Hannibal, my brother Benjamin had the impertinence to die, and my mother forced me to touch the dead boy's face. At age seven I walked into my father's room late one night and found a dead man looking at me; some fool had imprudently gotten himself stabbed. My father was the local judge, and authorized to investigate murders, so I suppose the corpse had come to see him on official business, rather than a social call. We often had cadavers stopping by to visit us of an evening, round about the dinner-hour. When I was eight, I saw a man get murdered right in front of me, and I watched the coroner dismantle him on my father's table. All callers at Chateau Clemens could be sure of finding a hot meal put together on the stove, and a cold corpse taken apart on the table. And one night when I was eleven, by God, the dead man on the table was *my father*, and I watched the coroners dissect *him* and haul the parts away for scrap. When I was seventeen, I slaughtered a man through my own bull-headed stupidity: gave some lucifer-matches to a half-crazy drunkard, and he used them to turn himself into an alcohol-lamp. He burned to death. Well, Missouri was knee-deep in corpses by then, so I lit out for the territory. Became a riverboat clerk, then a steersman, then a full pilot. My

GWYNPLAINE

younger brother Henry — my dearest brother, my favorite — came along with me at my insistence. Well, the Mississippi River came to kill him one night. But before it could take Henry, I murdered him."

"Henry Clemens was not murdered," said Thomas Twain, the hunch-backed dwarf. "He received a fatal dose of morphine, and . . ."

"Yes, goddamn you," said Mark Twain. "And *I gave it to him*. After our riverboat's boiler exploded, and Henry was scalded by the steam, *I* forced an inexperienced medical student to dose my brother with morphia. The intern had sense enough to admit his unwisdom . . . but I thought I knew better, and Henry died for it. So the river and I were quits from then on. I got married, settled down in New York, began a family, and proceeded to murder my son."

"I would hardly call that murder," said the moss-covered alternate Twain. "Langdon Clemens succumbed to diphtheria."

"Yes, he did," said Mark Twain. "And if you know that, then you know that *his death was the consequence of my deliberate actions*."

I waited for Twain's *Doppelgänger* to deny this . . . but the creature said nothing.

"Shall I count for you the corpses on parade?" Mark Twain asked. "The procession of frauds? My business failings, my loss of millions? My plunge into bankruptcy through bad speculations is well-known. *It is my own fault.* My favorite daughter Susy died in New York while I was hiding from my debts here in England. *My fault.* My wife, my darling Livy, died in Italy where I was cowering from my creditors. *My fault.* And my daughter Jean drowned one Christmas Eve, in my bathtub at Stormfield, and one hell of a Christmas present *that* was. *All my fault*."

"*There is no need to relive these passings*," said the dwarf-thing Thomas Twain, very gently. "*I have already seen them, mind-brother. I have shared your sadness, witnessed your sorrows, every moment from birth to your death. I have touched your whole life . . .*"

"*My life*, you thieving jackass!" Samuel Clemens jumped up, gripped Thomas Twain by the throat, and made a creditable attempt to strangle him. I gave a shout and ran towards them, and I promptly collided nose-first with some sort of invisible wall. I could not find an opening in it. The invisible barrier surrounded the two halves of the Twain; an impenetrable wall surrounding both, and keeping me out.

"*My life*, you damned jimjam buffoon!" Mark Twain howled, as he clutched his *Doppelgänger*. "Why, you thimble-riggin', pearl-buttoned, copper-bottomed, barrel-bellied, never-knew-the-territory *rube!* You were dead cargo, Tom. You stowed aboard Samuel Clemens and hid, shared my life without sharing the risks, spied on all my private secrets, watched my shames, saw my mistakes, and let *me* do all the galley-work. I piloted Sam Clemens all his bilgewater life, and I struck every rock, scraped every shallow, lost the compass overboard, hurt every person I cared about, and in general made every possible mistake . . . yes, and carried your stowaway carcass besides! You had the best end of the partnership, Tom: when I did anything right, you benefited from my success, but whenever I did something wrong I got stuck with all the blame and the responsibility. *You* never had to choose between the difficult virtue and the comfortable sin, Tom; *you* never had to fight, or bleed, or work at something for back-breaking years and watch it explode in your face. Hell, the only face *you* ever wore is *mine!* I never wanted to be Samuel Langhorne Claimants; it's a losing proposition. But who else could I be? *Mark Twain?* I never owned that name; I stole it from a decent honest man: Isaiah Sellers. No matter how much success I might find as 'Mark Twain', the world still knew I'd plundered that identity. I made a failure of Clemens, and I never earned the right to be Mark Twain. *So now who shall I be, brother Thomas?*"

I saw what was happening, but I was unable to stop it.

"I wanted to trade places with you," whispered Clemens, while he strangled his brother. The misshapen thing he'd christened Thomas Twain shook and quivered in his grip, its eyeballs bulging horribly. The star-twin visitor was apparently unable to change back from solid flesh to its energy form, because it struggled yet could not break free.

"I wanted us to horse-trade, brother Tom," Samuel Clemens crooned to the thing in his hands, while he lovingly tightened his stranglehold. *"As I told my daughter Clara on my deathbed: you and I, brother Tom, we were Jekyll and Hyde, but I never figured out which one of us was which. I wanted you to be Sam Clemens for a while, to see if you'd do any better in the pilot-house than I did, while I could sit in your place on the passenger deck. I wanted to give you the chaw and take back the plug. And if you piloted Clemens's life just as badly as I did, IT WOULD NOT BE MY FAULT . . ."*

"For God's sake, man, *stop it!*" I shouted. "You're *killing* him!" I tried again to restrain Clemens, to rescue his brother, but the barrier held; I was unable to touch them.

132

Thomas Twain suddenly gasped; I heard a snap, and then his head tumbled backwards on its neck. Clemens let go of him and Thomas Twain fell, his grotesque deformed body twitching spasmodically. After a time he stopped moving, and Clemens and I watched him in silence.

"Right. That's it, then," I said to the murderer. *"Now* what?"

"And now, if you'll excuse me," said Samuel Clemens, relighting his cigar with another hot coal while he helped himself to some more of my brandy, "I must be off. I'm late for work."

"What sort of work?" I asked of him.

"Oh, I make myself useful," said Mark Twain. "You've no doubt heard of the ferryman Charon, who ferried the souls of the damned to Hades across the river Styx. Well, old Charlie — as we call him — had to give up the job a few years back, on account of his chilblains; he couldn't take the damp. So the Superintendent of Hell — yes, the Publisher and Editor-in-Chief of the place — offered Charlie a job closer to the fire, and advertised for a new ferry captain, preferably with piloting experience. I assured him that, after wrestling the Mississippi for so many years, I could navigate the Styx blindfolded. Then I slipped Brother Satan five dollars, and he gave me the job. I am the new riverboat captain on the Styx Line to Hell, sir — departures hourly, one-way passages for all, children travel half-price, group rates for Congressmen and bank presidents, no round-trip tickets obtainable — and if you plan on relocating to Hell, sir . . . for I seem to recall seeing your name on one of our upcoming passenger lists . . . I will gladly reserve you a seat on the observation deck, near the pilot-house."

"Not just yet, thanks," I said. "I'm still hoping for an upper berth in Heaven, although I am told that Hell offers far more extensive entertainment facilities. I believe that Heaven is a better address than Hell: the rent is cheaper, and the plumbing works. And I see no particular reason why I should suffer the eternal torments of Hell, since I have already spent three days in San Francisco."

"Suit yourself," Mark Twain shrugged. "Angels' wings don't appeal to me, though. I'm allergic to feathers."

"On your way out," I said, "please dispose of this corpse you've deposited on my carpet, and . . ."

I stopped. The cadaver of Thomas Twain had disappeared. I looked up again, to confront Samuel Clemens, but in the instant in which I had looked away from him the fellow had vanished. On the far wall, a window that I had shut was now open and letting in the cold air of the Februaried London. I heard a sound in the distance just then, like the call of a steam whistle.

I went to the window and looked. It was a dark night, with not even a toenail-paring of moon, but — by the receding glow of Halley's Comet as it sped away from Earth — I saw, or thought I saw, a dark shape moving down the Thames, towards Chelsea Bridge. In the dimness and distance I could not be certain, but it looked like a paddlewheel steamboat.*

Although I regretted the death of Thomas Twain, I still felt some relief that he and his counterpart brother were gone. "I'm glad *that's* over with," I thought, half-aloud. "Now perhaps I can get . . ."

"Excuse me," said the floor lamp.

One seldom knows what reply to make to floor lamps . . . or to light bulbs, rather, since the voice had emanated from a light bulb in the top of the lamp. After considering several pithy japes on the order of "Watt are you and wire you in my ohm?" or "Yes, my precious, coulomb, coulomb!" I discarded them, and made a statement much more to the point: "Um, er, ah, well, that is . . ."

"Oh, pardon. Is it safe to come out?" A fragment of light detached itself from the glow of the light bulb's filament, passed through the glass shell of the bulb, and hovered near the fireplace. *"It's me again,"* said the comet-wanderer.

"Thomas Twain?" I asked. "I thought that Clemens had killed you."

"The reports of my death," said the glimmer of light, *"have been greatly . . ."*

"Never mind. Why did you come here?"

"I have spent," said the visitor, *"nearly seventy-six of your planet's years on Earth, within Clemens's mind. I was unable to leave Earth, but gradually I came to like the place. You humans are an interesting species, despite your regrettable peculiarities."*

"Thank you," I said. "We try our best to amuse interstellar visitors."

---

* At this juncture some knowledgeable reader will point out that Chelsea Bridge — although within walking distance of Mark Twain's London home — cannot be seen from Tedworth Square, and that — on the morning of 9 February 1986 — Halley's Comet as viewed from Earth was in the southern constellation Aquila, and therefore could not be observed from London's 51°30' north latitude position.

There is, however, a very simple and obvious explanation, which I shall gladly reveal as soon as I think of it.

(The above footnote appeared in the original version of this story, in 1986. I still haven't thought of an explanation yet.)

134

"And it is lonely out there, in the voidness of space. My vessel Star-Mother contains me, nurtures me during the sleep between the stars, but this is never enough. I seek companionship."

"Are there no others of your people?" I asked.

"The wanderers? Man, there are many thousand-millions of us! But it chances so seldom that two comets pass close to one another. Most of the time, for the long many years when our comet-ships ride free between worlds, my people sleep. But when I dwelt on Earth, in the mind of Samuel Clemens, I was alive, and knew other minds, and tasted pleasures and life!"

I was beginning to understand. "And so now that Halley's Comet brought you close to Earth again, you . . ."

"Oh, human-born man, have you never been homesick? I have not tasted this world for many severals of years . . . not since your year 1910. I could not resist one more visit . . . a brief one, this time, as I soon must return to Star-Mother. But for now . . . well, as Mark Twain almost said once: When one has been absent from a planet for seventy-six years, there is much news to learn when one comes back."

"When you arrived in my rooms earlier this evening," I asked, "why did you pretend to be Mark Twain?"

"I knew no other form I might inhabit as well as his. Besides, he had often wanted me to take a turn at being Samuel Clemens to see how painful it was."

"Was that really Mark Twain," I asked, "who returned here just now?"

"It was the part of him, I think, that held his madness," said my visitor. "Did he really come here tonight from Hell? I don't know; such districts are beyond my province. I think perhaps that, when Mark Twain lived in this house in Tedworth Square, in 1896, some part of his dementia — the fear of his own mind's dual nature, the agony of a man who hid from his creditors while his daughter died alone — was so strong that it permeated the walls of this place, and it waited and ripened and grew, until it burst forth tonight. You grasp the concept that this entails?"

"Glub," I responded. "Well, no, I don't quite understand it, but it'll probably sneak up on me when I'm not looking. I say, what was that invisible thing I bumped into? That barrier surrounding you and Clemens?"

"I did that," said the comet-born one. "A simple stasis of photons. Any infant could do it with fifty years' practice. I didn't want you to interfere when Samuel Clemens killed me."

"What, you *wanted* him to kill . . ."

"I wanted him to do whatever was necessary for him to find peace. And if changing myself into physical matter, and allowing him to destroy what he perceived as his mind's darker self would bring him peace, I was willing to do it. And yet I had hoped, after so long an absence, that he would greet me more warmly. For I dwelt in his mind for more than seventy years, and I loved him."

"Like a brother, of course," I suggested.

"No. Something more. You see, Samuel Clemens called me 'Thomas', but I think that perhaps a more suitable name would have been . . ." the visitor paused, *". . . Tamsyn, or even Thomasina."*

Then the visitor came forward, in a glistening of light, and I felt her touch my mind. There was a warmth upon my forehead and my face, like sunlight's whispering . . . but it was light that came from far beyond the sun, for the comet in her interstellar flight had harvested light from distant stars. And for a moment she was present within me, and I within her. Then the thought spoke: *"Farewell,"* and I saw the dancing light approach my window. *"Star-Mother beckons."*

The visitor was gone. But I looked out the window and saw, far in distance away, in the sky above Battersea Bridge, the blazing light of Halley's Comet as it drew away from Earth. And the sight was so magnificent that, as I witnessed it, I held one precious thought: *There simply MUST be some way I can make a buck out of this. . . .*

And then I was alone. I heard the bells of Saint Luke's Church, in Sydney Street just across the way, striking seven; and I realised that the night was over, and it was nearly dawn. The sun sneaked out from behind Chelsea Barracks, buttoning its trousers and looking rather pleased with itself after having been out all night.

"Is that the last of it, then?" I asked the floor lamp. "No more extra-terrestrials setting up light housekeeping in your lampshade, I trust? Well, wall? Any poltergeists in your pinewood panels, perchance? Hullo, armchair: any apparitions in your upholstery, then? I say there, television: got any ghosts for me? Any banshees taken up lodgings in your videorthicon thingummy? Any ghouls, any ghasts, any goblins today? Speak up, spooks: any spectres to speak of? What? None whatever?"

Silence.

"Remarkable," I said. "I do believe that I'm well and truly alone at last. I wonder if . . ."

The door burst open, and a hideous thing staggered forth. *"In God's name, sir, help me!"* it screeched.

The intruder was apparently a man, but his form was so haggard and gaunt that he seemed to be more skeletal than human. His clothes were filthy rags, his long grey beard was entangled with bits of leaves and dried blood. His entire body was thickly encrusted with every imaginable sort of filth, and the very odour of his flesh filled the room with so odious a stench that for a moment I mistook him for my publishing agent. The cadaverous intruder collapsed on my doorstep, rasping fitfully, his tongue swollen with thirst. There was dust in the wrinkles of his face, and his eyes — blue, flecked reddish with bloodshot — were grown wide with the sight of unknown horrors.

"Some brandy, for charity's sake!" he pleaded, and I ran to fetch a glassful. He consumed it greedily. "Many thanks, friend," he coughed, and I swear there was dust in his throat.

I gave him the rest of the bottle. "I never imagined," he gasped, between draughts, "that when those Aztec priests forced me to ingest their immortality elixir, it would take me seventy-two years to escape."

"Aztec priests?" I asked, picking up the nearest blunt instrument, and coming towards him. "Immortality elixir? *Seventy-two years?"*

"That is correct," said the dust-covered man. "I am the war correspondent for the Washington *American*. The name's Bierce, Ambrose Bierce, and . . ."

I let out a screech that must have rattled window-panes in Stoke Newington as I grabbed the old wretch by the seat of his neck and the scruff of his trousers, and I pitched him headlong down the stairs. He landed butt-over-appetite, hurtled over the doorstep, and scurried off into the darkness whence he had come. *One* literary loony per week is quite enough for me just at present, thanks, and I hope that's the end of them. But I plan on sleeping with a contraband Heckler & Koch modified full-automatic pistol tucked under my pillow from now on, just in case H. P. Lovecraft shows up some dark night, selling tickets for the Second Coming of Chthulhu. I mean, *really!*

Although I started writing professionally in the 1960s, most of my early efforts were hackwork novels written under pseudonyms. But when I wrote 'Martian Walkabout', I fancied it enough to put my right name to it. After it was published in *Isaac Asimov's Science Fiction Magazine* in 1980, Terry Carr selected it for inclusion in one of his prestigious **Best Science Fiction of the Year** anthologies.

'Martian Walkabout' is one of my more personal efforts. I was brought to Australia from Scotland during the *child migrant* scheme of the postwar years. I spent part of my early life — I have difficulty thinking of it as a 'childhood' — in orphanages in rural Australia, such as the Mapoon Mission Station Industrial School and the Westbrook Farm Home for Boys. Some of my cellmates in these institutions were aborigine children. When I was older, I lived and worked with aborigines in various regions of the Australian outback: sometimes in cattle or sheep stations, sometimes on tribal lands. I became fascinated with the aboriginal conceptions of time and memory, of reality and dreams: these are utterly different from our 'whitefella' perceptions of these concepts.

The hero of 'Martian Walkabout' is named Kundekundeka: this would translate as *'tooth-tooth-birth'*, and it's an appropriate name for a male child born with two teeth. In the aboriginal culture, to be born with a tooth is a sign that one has been favoured by the gods: a child born with *two* teeth is clearly destined for great things.

'Martian Walkabout' proves that I can't predict the future with 100% accuracy. When I wrote this story in 1979, Ayers Rock was administered by the Australian government, and aborigines were kept away from the ancestral sites surrounding that monolith. I assumed that these circumstances would prevail into the twenty-first century, until the time when we begin to colonise Mars. But in 1985 — after this story was first published — the Australian government restored Ayers Rock to the indigenous people, who now lease it as a tourist attraction (I got *that* bit right!) to the National Parks and Wildlife Service.

When I wrote 'Martian Walkabout', I kept to a bare minimum the aboriginal words and cultural terms in the story, because I wanted to avoid alienating American readers who did not recognise these terms. In hindsight, I realise that this was a mistake: for this revised version, I have deepened the aboriginal aspects of the story. I've also updated some details of Martian cartography.

I confess that I've invented several details of aboriginal culture to fit the needs of my story. Although Ayers Rock is indeed sacred to the aborigines of the central outback, they do not normally *climb* the monolith, for the same reason that Anglicans don't usually climb Westminster Abbey: that's not what it's for. Also, the song-myths of the *Wandjina* spirits are not indigenous to the central outback where this story takes place. The *Wandjina* cult belongs to the Ngarinyin people and other tribes of the West Kimberley language group, many hundreds of miles west of Ayers Rock. To place *Wandjina* at Ayers Rock is rather like attributing Amerindian totem poles to the Sioux. I was aware of this error when I wrote 'Martian Walkabout', yet I chose to carry on regardless. If the inaccuracies bother you, you can pretend that 'Martian Walkabout' takes place in an alternate-universe Australia, where I've got all the details correct.

I continue to be deeply interested in the many different aboriginal cultures of Australia. **The Mammoth Book of Historical Detectives**, a British anthology published in 1995, contains a story I wrote titled 'Death in the Dawntime': this is a murder mystery set in 40,000 BC, among the prehistoric Wuradjeri people of southeastern Australia. That story has some science-fictional elements, but I tried to keep it accurate in its depiction of the Wuradjeri. I'm currently writing a novel about the song-myths and culture of the Nunggubooyoo people in the northern outback.

Just now, though, I give you 'Martian Walkabout'.

MARTIAN WALKABOUT

Originally published in *Isaac Asimov's Science Fiction Magazine*, March 1980.

There are two edges to reality, son of my son: each as different from the other as night is from day. There is the Wakingworld, and then there is the Dreamtime. In the Dreamtime, all times and all places are one, and every corner of the universe touches every other. And remember, my child, that when the Dreamtime commands, then you must *obey. For it is in the Dreamtime that we will dance among the stars . . .*

When Kundekundeka was five, his grandfather Ramijirring told him legends of the Dreamtime and beyond. On a summer night, while the tribe gathered in the ritual of *corroborree*, while the moon glistened mystically over the waters of the distant billabong, and while the silver skyships of the whitefellas drifted overhead, Ramijirring sang the time-songs.

He sang of Kunapipi, the feathered she-serpent of the far-distant Dreamtime, who created men from the grass and women from the sand, and saw them multiply across the desert outback. He told of Jangardbla, the red-haired warrior who slew a hundred enemies with his strong left hand, and who conquered the beast-men of Luritja. And he told of the people *Wandjina*, who came from the stars and went back to them, in the days of our grandfathers' grandfathers, and who wore lightning in their hair. The *Wandjina* had no mouths, for they held all the weather of the world within themselves . . . and if they spoke, tempests and tidal waves would run out of their faces and drown the whole Earth. All these things were many rains ago, in the days of *Kutjulpitu*: in the Big Walktime when the coolibah groves whispered magic, and the Bunyip sang, and the enchanted *Miruru* spirits rode the high wind. But then came the *walypalu* — the whitefellas — and they brought with them their guns and horses and fences. The *walypalu* said that this place Woombalooru was now part of some land called Australia, and on that day the magic left Woombalooru forever.

When Kundekundeka was nine, his grandfather Ramijirring taught him how to play the wooden drum and the *ebroo* tree-flute, and then — when Kundekundeka had mastered these — his grandfather taught him to play the most beautiful instrument of all: the didjeridoo. Ten feet long and as thick as a man's arm it was, but Kundekundeka never forgot how it sang silver notes when his grandfather breathed life into it:

OOdaOOdaOOdadadaOOROOdadaOOROOdaah . . . !

When Kundekundeka was twelve, the time came for his entry into manhood. His grandfather Ramijirring taught him how to use the woomera and the spear and the knife. He taught him which beasts were taboo and which ones might safely be hunted. He taught Kundekundeka how to forage for *mingkiri*: any of the non-taboo small animals that were suitable for food. Kundekundeka learnt how to hunt Ninoo the bandicoot, and how to bring down the kangaroo Nyatunya with one throw of the curved-stick boonang, and how to make the boonang fly back to his hand when he tossed it into the wind. And Ramijirring taught his grandson how to use *Wirtit*: the bull-roarer, the flat stick on a braided-hair thong that could sing to the spirits and let them know that the hunting was good.

"Always remember, *tjamu-tju*, my grandson," Ramijirring would say, "that you are a member of the tribe Woombalooru, the most noble of nations. And we the tribe Woombalooru are the favoured ones, for we are watched over by the spirits who dwell in mighty Oolooru, the Stone-from-the-Sky. Sacred is Oolooru above all else."

Oftentimes, on a steaming summer night, while the men of the tribe did their snake-dance to the throb of the didjeridoo, young Kundekundeka could look southwards and see Oolooru looming on the desert horizon. He asked his aged grandfather why the people Woombalooru spent their days wandering, instead of living peacefully in the shade of Oolooru. And Ramijirring replied:

"Nowadays no man among us goes there, but in my day Oolooru was home. Shall I tell you what the place was like, child? Rock and sand and little else, but if you can climb the rocky peaks of Oolooru as I did once, aye, and reach the very centre of the crest you shall find the Valley of Oolooru. And there grow trees and birds and grasses, and the waters are sweet. In the Valley of Oolooru, son of my son, far away from mortal eyes."

Kundekundeka was silent, and for a moment he sat and listened to the throb of the didjeridoo:

OOdaOOdaOOdadadaOOROOdadaOOROOdaah . . . !

"But why have we strayed from Oolooru, grandfather? Why may we never see the Valley of Oolooru?"

"Because the whitefellas came with their petrol and their sugar and flour, and their National Heritage Trust," said Ramijirring scornfully. "They came here with their dollars and sunglasses and their big gods Coca-Cola and Polaroid, and they chased us away from our homeland Oolooru." The old man's eyes misted as he spoke. "They call the place Ayers Rock now, I think."

Kundekundeka was silent, and in the stillness of night the didjeridoo played more loudly.

When Kundekundeka was thirteen he became a man. The ritual-spear *ngaltawata* was thrust upright into the ground, to signify that this was a men-place, where female observers were forbidden. Two Woombalooru tribesmen held Kundekundeka down while the tribe's Doctor Man circumcised him with a Wilkinson Sword razor blade. Kundekundeka was determined not to cry out during the ordeal, lest he shame the spirits of mighty Oolooru. But the pain was too great, and he screamed. Afterwards, burning with pain, he crept alone through the speargrass to a place where none could see him behold Oolooru on the twilight horizon. "I have been unworthy, Oolooru," he whispered to the looming monolith. "But I shall make it up to you, in the time of walkabout."

And the huge sandstone shape heard him, and changed from orange to red to purple, by way of showing that it understood.

Then came the sunrise of *Yalatja*: the Walkabout dawn.

Kundekundeka and each of the other young males stood proudly as the elders addressed them. Each youth stood, some naked and some with loincloth and one in Levi dungarees, and each one took the weapon of his choosing. Kundekundeka chose the knife, and took a bull-roarer as well, so that the spirits would know if his hunting was good.

He set out towards the east with two other lads. After three walklongs he tarried, and let the other two go on without him. Kundekundeka took a branch from an ironbark tree and he whittled this into *wana*, his digging-stick. Then he squatted, and probed the brittle saltpan surfaces for *purara*, the honey-ants. He ate three manygrabs of these, all the while squinting towards the distant outback horizon as the figures of the other two boys became smaller and far. At last, when he was finally alone, Kundekundeka stood up again. He licked the syrup of the honey-ants from his fingers, and reclaimed his knife. Now he turned, and began travelling *yulparira* — southwards — towards Oolooru. Towards the Stone-from-Sky.

Suddenly in the distance he heard a didjeridoo playing, mocking him with its voice, and he froze: was this a good omen or bad? He squinted towards Oolooru, and at that instant the angry red monolith turned a friendly shade of yellow as the sun climbed over its eastern rim.

A good omen. Kundekundeka gripped the knife in his teeth, and broke into a run towards the peak. Towards the Valley of Oolooru, where the waters were sweet. And if the Valley was there, then he — Kundekundeka — was going to find it.

*   *   *

"Ayers Rock," said the tour guide. "One single massive sandstone, the largest rock found anywhere on Earth. Fourteen hundred feet high, and five miles round at its base. Why, it covers more ground than the City of London!"

A plump lady held up her hand. "But isn't this aboriginal land? I thought there were abos living on the peak of the rock."

"Not quite," said the tour guide while several holocams flashed. "The indigenous tribe never had a permanent settlement here — they were nomads, y'see — but this was one of their ritual places, more than a century ago. When we get a bit farther on, you'll see paintings on the rock: aboriginal paintings where they mixed the ochre paint with their own blood. Some sort of mumbo-jumbo sacrament, I'll be bound. Every now and again, some abo would show up here and cut himself, trying to freshen up the rock art with a bit of his own blood supply. So we had to make them scarper off away from here."

A skinny man, with absolutely no hair, spoke up: "Why's this place so sacred to the aborigines, then?"

"The abos believe that Ayers Rock came from outer space . . . or whatever their word is for *heaven*. They actually believe that, many years ago, Ayers Rock fell out of the sky and landed here, in the middle of nowhere. I'm glad I wasn't standing here when it happened." Several members of the tour group chuckled, and their guide continued: "Load of rubbish, of course. Geologists have confirmed that Ayers Rock is a natural sandstone formation, as old as the Earth.

Not from outer space at all. The rock is coated with iron oxide . . . from erosion, y'see . . . and its colour changes are caused by the sun's rays refracting through the hot desert air."

In a shadowed grove of kurrajong trees, Kundekundeka watched. He had formed a plan as he came walkabout here *kayili-nguru*, from the north. It was late afternoon now; he wanted to reach the Valley of Oolooru before moonrise. Kundekundeka edged warily towards the superhighway stretching between him and Oolooru; he had never seen asphalt or macadam before, and Kundekundeka was certain that the whitefellas' road would feel horribly alien beneath his toes.

His foot touched the road, and at that instant he heard the distant drone of a didjeridoo: *OOdaOOda*. Kundekundeka jumped back as if he'd been stabbed. Overhead, mighty Oolooru suddenly turned magenta, in anger.

Too late to turn back. There were no white men here now. Kundekundeka took a deep breath, stuck his knife between his jaws and raced across the roadway towards an overhang of the sandstone monolith. A mighty leap, brown fingers scrabbling for a grip, and then he was up. He, Kundekundeka, son of the Woombalooru, had returned to the home of his people!

OOdaOOdaOOdadadaOOROOdadaOOROOdaah . . . !

He climbed. Even in the afternoon that was turning to evening it was blistering hot, and the sweat rolled off Kundekundeka in rivulets. At last, high on the northern face of the huge sandstone, he came to a broad grooved hollow slope that was rippled and wrinkled like the surface of a gigantic brain, and here he rested for a time. He was still gasping for breath when he suddenly heard footsteps behind him.

The old man was a whitefella, but the sun had made him nearly as bronze-skinned as Kundekundeka. The wary youth was too exhausted to stand up as the dark-skinned *walypala* man came closer.

"You speak English, lad?"

Kundekundeka remained silent.

"No worries, mate; you can trust me. I'm dinkum. My name's Lofty. You get lost or something?"

Kundekundeka sat up with an effort. His knife was lying near his hand, between two grooves of the enormous sandstone brain, and he wondered if he could reach for his weapon without provoking an attack. It is a well-known truth that all the whitefellas have guns . . .

Lofty took a step towards him, then stopped as the youth's body tensed. "Look here, cobber, I live on this rock. The Heritage pays me, y'know. If you're lost, I can help you get home. But if you're just huntin' for bush tucker, then you'll have to do it someplace else. Right, so what's it to be?"

Off in the distance a whine, a thrum of gathering power. Kundekundeka looked and saw a strange flying machine coming towards him, parallel to the crest of Oolooru. He reached for his knife, and gripped it hard.

"That's just the whirlybird, lad. You'll be right. That there 'copter can land on the Rock, though it's not meant to. You want a ride back down? Be somethin' to tell your brothers and sisters about, over the . . ."

Kundekundeka broke into a run, slipping past the man Lofty and on up the slope towards the summit. A stand of high speargrass growing here, a clump of spinifex there, growing from the sandstone; he used the vegetation for cover as he ran. He took advantage of the growing darkness as the sun set. Helter-skelter he ran, not straight on, but dingo-crafty: changing directions to dodge his pursuers, but always rushing by angles and turns towards his goal with the sweat pouring out of his flesh, and the blood vessels pounding in his eardrums . . .

OOdaOOdaOOdadadaOOROOdadaOOROOdaah . . . !

A shadow dropped out of the sky, hovering above him like some winged carrion-eater, and Kundekundeka looked up and saw the flying machine. He screeched in dismay and defiance, ran faster, ducked beneath an overhang where the flying machine could not see him, and he raced towards the crest of Oolooru while the chant of the didjeridoo went mad inside his brain . . .

OOdaOOdaOOROOdada . . . !

Nearly there, a few more runalongs. He risked a glance backwards and saw the white man Lofty puffing right behind him. "*Hi!* Stop there, you! We won't hurt you, sonny, but you've got to get off Ayers Rock!"

"Oolooru!" gasped Kundekundeka as he ran. An alien face flashed past him: red and blue it was with much yellow, and even as he ran Kundekundeka recognised the long eyes and the vertical slit of a nose with no mouth underneath: the face of the *Wandjina*, the sky-beings, painted on the sandstone wall one night many centuries past. He was nearing the Valley of Oolooru!

OOdaOOdaOOROOdada . . . !

The flying machine swooped down upon him, like Kuniya the she-python snatching her prey. Kundekundeka turned, dodged, ran faster, and then in the last

145

fading glow of desert twilight he scrambled to the crest of the ridge and looked down to see what lay beyond.

The Valley of Oolooru!

The flying machine was right over him now. The boy fled its chuddering blades. With his eyes towards the valley, Kundekundeka raced across the bare upper face of the sandstone, ever closer to the lush green foliage that beckoned him downhill. Another few steps, another few steps, *OOdaOOda*, and then — on the very edge of the mystic valley — sudden white fingers gripped him and sunburnt white hands pinned his arms, and then sullen white men were dragging him up the hillside towards the flying machine.

"Oolooru!" sobbed Kundekundeka. Then the air shimmered in the outback's heat, and in an instant the valley was gone.

"Crazy abos," Lofty grunted. "Always tryin' to do their clever-clevers on the bleedin' rock. Look sharp, Robbo! This blackie's a right wild 'un."

The last thing Kundekundeka saw before they dragged him away was the sky full of stars, and suddenly he remembered his grandfather's tales of the *Wandjina*, who came from the stars and went back to them, in the days beyond the Dreamtime. The stars overhead now were *tiwa tjura*, distant fires: so many tiny silver gleams far away in the sky, and near the horizon one speck of light that gleamed red like the outback desert, and which somehow seemed much closer than the other distant gleams. For a long moment Kundekundeka wondered which of those tiny lights in the sky was the *Wandjina* homeland, and then suddenly nothing mattered anymore.

OOdaOOdaOOdadadaOOROOdadaOOROOdaah . . . !

*　　*　　*

"You want to *what?*" screeched Arnstein. After ten years in the Service he'd have sworn that nothing could surprise him anymore, but right now he was getting the surprise of his career.

"I want to stay behind," the tall brown-skinned crewman repeated. "Here on Mars, with only a spear and a knife. The ship can return to Earth without me, and there'll be another ship coming for me in three months' time."

"You're crazy," said the mission commander. "I'd have booted you out of the Service a long time ago, if you weren't the best astrogator I've ever served

147

with. What's this walkabout nonsense, anyway?"

Johnny Kundekundeka Longfellow, which was the name the whitefellas had saddled him with when he'd joined the Service, drew himself up to full height as he spoke: "The walkabout — the Yalatja — is one of the sacred rituals of Woombalooru. It is one man's attempt to triumph over a hostile environment. When a boy becomes a man, he sets out alone in the desert. If he comes back alive, he has proven worthy of manhood. If not, well . . ."

Mission Commander Arnstein grunted. "And you figured you'd wait until you got to Mars to walkabout, hey?"

"No, sir; I did my walkabout on Earth, but I failed and I was brought home in disgrace by the *walypalu.*"

"Pardon?"

"Sorry, commander. The term *'walypalu'* is derived from my ancestors' first attempt to pronounce the word *'European'*. It means . . . the whitefellas. After my dishonour, I could not face my Woombalooru kinsmen, so I went to live among the white people."

Arnstein stepped over to the starboard bulkhead and he switched on the ventilator. Outside the viewport, looking west across the Tharsis mountain range to the Martian horizon, he could see the terraform crew returning to the ship: their faces masked by breathing apparatus, their bodies glowing an eerie red in the light of the distant volcano Pavonis Mons. "I still don't see why you're so eager to commit suicide," he said.

"Sir, are you familiar with the ways of Woombalooru? Our most sacred possession is our *Tjukurpa.*"

"What's that when it's at home, then?"

"The concept has no whitefella equivalent. In my homeland Woombalooru, every beast and plant and waterhole and stone has its own song-myth, its legend: the chant of its soul. The *Tjukurpa.* I have my own *Tjukurpa,* which I must not chant in your presence lest you commit song-theft and copy my soul. My *Tjukurpa* does not live inside me, for it dwells within the Dreamtime."

Arnstein looked slightly relieved. "I've heard of *that* one, at least. Saw an article about the aboriginal Dreamtime in a magazine once, back when magazines were still printed on paper."

Johnny Kundekundeka Longfellow nodded. "In the seventeen years that I have lived among your people, I have often sung of the Dreamtime. It is the other edge of time, the other side of reality: where our souls go while our bodies sleep. My people hold our dreams and our nightmares to be of vital importance."

Arnstein started to grunt again, then thought better of it. "So?"

"Most dreams, commander, are omens of a sort: warnings or predictions of some major event. So says Woombalooru lore. But last night, sir, when I came back to the ship after assisting the surveying team . . . last night, while I slept in my quarters, breathing Martian air through Terran converters, I had a dream that took the shape of a *command*."

"What did it say?"

"It did not speak to me: it *sang*." Kundekundeka's eyes were shining. "The dream sang to me, commanding me to do walkabout again. To succeed, when before I had failed. I *must* do walkabout on Mars."

"Do your people who flunk walkabout the first time generally get a second chance?" Arnstein asked.

"Never, sir. It has never been done. But neither has a son of Woombalooru ever trod the Martian sands before. Last night, the Dreamtime sang that I must not fail my second walkabout, because there will be no hope of rescue. After this ship leaves without me tomorrow, I'll be alone on Mars until the next expedition arrives in three months."

"Let me get this straight," said the commander, glancing towards the viewport again. The surveying team were aboard now, and Arnstein could see the sun hanging low above the Martian hills; he'd better end this discussion fast or he'd be late for evening chow call. "You want me to dump you outside, butt-naked, with no supplies and no chance of rescue? On the red desert of *Mars?*"

"My homeland too is a red desert," said Kundekundeka.

"Damn it, man, that's not Australia outside the viewport! We're on Mars: *Mars*, as in sub-polar nightfall and toxic dust storms! I'll admit that the last few years of terraforming missions have made the temperature a bit warmer and the atmosphere a bit more oxygenated, but this is still *an alien planet. . .*"

"I have spent the past seventeen years on an alien planet," said Kundekundeka. *"Your* world, commander, the world of the white men is alien to me. Mars is not alien."

"Mars has damned little biosphere and no life-forms bigger than microbes," Arnstein reminded him. "With both hands and a miracle, you might just possibly find water, but what about *food?*"

149

"The desert will provide," said Kundekundeka. "My dream-song did not mention food, so perhaps my walkabout will not require food."

"And you're doing this because a *dream* told you to?"

Kundekundeka nodded. "It sounds foolish to you, I know. But when the Dreamtime commands, the Woombalooru obey. I would not receive a dream of this nature unless there were some vital purpose behind it. That is my religion, sir. I could point out characteristics of your own religion that seem just as foolish to . . ."

"Damn it, religion is one thing, but you're talking about *suicide!* Request denied, Longfellow. Dismissed!"

Johnny Kundekundeka Longfellow went to the hatchway and turned. "When the Dreamtime speaks, then the Woombalooru obey. This ship leaves at 0817 hours tomorrow, commander. I will not be on board."

"You'll be on board and at your post if I have to *nail* you to it!" growled Arnstein. "We've lost our original launch window, and you're the only astrogations man aboard I can trust to get this crate back to Earth. I'll be damned if I maroon you on Mars and have your death on *my* Service record. Request denied, denied, and denied again. Dis-*missed!*"

These crazy foreigners, Arnstein thought as he made his way belowdecks for the evening mess call. *Oh well, maybe there'll be pie for dessert . . .*

*   *   *

Kundekundeka made one last safety check of the breathing apparatus and then fitted the respirator over his mouth and nose. He'd gone through quite a moral struggle before deciding that this oxygen device would not violate the basic strictures of his walkabout on Mars. In the traditional walkabouts of his youth in his homeland, such high-tech survival devices would have been forbidden . . . but, in the outback, such technology would have been unnecessary.

He shrugged himself into the jumpsuit, checked the air seals, and zipped it up: one more item that was vital to survival in the Martian climate. But from here on, it was strictly back-to-nature: no radio comlink, no medical supplies. He would leave the shelter of the spacecraft and the hastily-erected geodesic domes surrounding it, and search the nearby Martian hills for a *wilychta:* a cave or any feature of erosion that would offer him haven from the elements. He would need to forage for his water supply: if there even *was* enough water on this entire planet to sustain a man for three months. But surely the spirits of the Dreamtime would provide.

Kundekundeka ripped loose the emergency survival kit that was sewn into the jumpsuit's lining, and flung it aside, then he picked up the survival kit of the Woombalooru: a spear and a knife. He had brought these along on the journey to Mars among his personal effects, assuring the senior officers that these were implements deeply linked to his religious beliefs . . . as indeed they were. Now he hefted the curved-stick boonang (which the whitefellas insisted on calling a *boomerang*), and he wondered if it would soar through the air here on Mars as it did back on Earth. As a huntsman in the outback, he had learnt to throw the boonang so that it would unerringly return to his hand, providing he aimed it at his prey while facing into the wind . . . hardly a disadvantage, since any skilled huntsman will take care to approach his prey only from the downwind flank. Would the boonang return to him if he flung it into the savage winds on the outback of Mars? Kundekundeka took it along.

In the silence of his quarters the commander's words came back to him, and for a moment Kundekundeka thought that Arnstein was right: he *was* committing suicide. But no, that was ridiculous; had not the Dreamtime guided him wisely all his life? Why should it betray him now?

Silently, as befit a Woombalooru huntsman, he stalked along down the passageway to the airlock. The officer on duty was MacDonald. Disengaging his own respirator, Kundekundeka strode up jovially and waved to the older man.

"Got a little treat here, Mack." Johnny Kundekundeka Longfellow grinned broadly and held up two frosty cans of Victoria Bitter that he'd bartered out of the mess officer's stores. Keeping one can for himself, he pressed the other cold one into his friend's hand. "Here, have a drink. *Arkala tjikila.* That's Woombalooru lingo for 'Here, have a drink.'" Kundekundeka popped the first can open and raised it to his lips, pretending to drink. *"Alatji*: here's how."

MacDonald grinned and accepted the bribe. "Cheers, mate . . . though, if you don't mind, I'll save this till I'm off-duty."

Lifting his open can, Kundekundeka winked. "Me, I think I'll enjoy this outside. Sip a little beer and admire the view, eh?" He moved towards the airlock, hoping that MacDonald wouldn't think to ask him how he intended to drink a beer through his respirator.

"Fine with me, Johnny." MacDonald activated the airlock mechano, but then abruptly stopped. "Hey, what's with the spear, friend?"

"Eh? Oh, just thought I'd go outside and get a little target practice before curfew." The brown man grinned to his shipmate. "Who knows? Maybe I'll spear a Martian before he can zap me with his death-ray. Say, Mack, sing out my name at roll call tomorrow morning, will you? I'd like to skive a little extra sack-time."

"No worries, Johnny. Just remember to get back to the ship before we shove off tomorrow morning." MacDonald finished activating the airlock, then laughed. "Hey, wouldn't it be funny if you didn't get back here in time for our launch window, and we had to leave without you?"

*   *   *

The Martian wind bit hard into his face, and Kundekundeka hunched over and turned up the respirator. It suddenly occurred to him that he ought to go back and get a spare power cell, just in case his survival rig didn't have enough juice for the whole three months of . . .

No. On second thought he'd have to take that chance; he was supposed to survive the walkabout on Woombalooru wits, not *walyapalu* hardware.

Besides, wasn't it preordained that he *had* to survive? His *Tjukurpa*, his sacred dream-chant would never have told him to do walkabout in this place without some definite reason. And when the Dreamtime sings to a son of Woombalooru, then he *must* obey.

In the low Martian gravity a hundred metres were like nothing, and with long loping strides Kundekundeka had soon left the ship and the terraform domes far behind. The next terraforming expedition from Earth was scheduled to land almost 1800 kilometres east of here, in the pockmarked region of Martian craters named Xanthe Terra. He'd have to travel 20 kilometres per day — travelling by daylight only, to conserve the power cell in his hand beacon — and a Martian day had only nineteen more minutes of daylight than an Earth day.

He kept walking. On this small planet the horizon seemed too close, almost as if he could fall off the edge of Mars. The stars looked unfamiliar in a Martian sky, and of course the Southern Cross that he'd always used as a path-finding aid in the outback would be useless here, even if Kundekundeka could find it overhead . . . and he couldn't. But the ancient instincts were strong within his Woombalooru soul, and in no time Kundekundeka had plotted a course east-wards. Glancing back, he saw that already the ship from Earth had dropped out of view below the nearby western horizon, and . . .

OOdaOOdaOOROOdada . . .

Kundekundeka stopped dead in his tracks and felt the flesh crawl at the back of his neck. The sound of the didjeridoo was unmistakeable . . . and it was coming from the south: from the maze-like network of Martian canyons and chasms known as Noctis Labyrinthus.

OOdadadaOOROOdaah . . . !

As if in a trance he took a step towards the sound, then recovered his senses and turned towards the east, then back again to the south. What was wrong? What the hell was he doing out here anyway? The ship! Get back to the ship, man, before they leave without you! This was crazy, sneaking out here like this *OOdaOOda* go east! No, south, damn it! Noise in my *OOda* west, in the *OOdaOOda* look at *OOROOdadaOOROOdada . . .*

The sound was undeniable, cutting into his brain like a spear, throbbing until he thought his eardrums would split *OOdaOOda*. The sound beckoned him to turn *yulparira*: southwards, towards Oolooru. No, that was back on Earth, and years ago. Kundekundeka turned and ran, pounded hard through the red dust of Mars until he suddenly stopped and cried out:

"Oolooru!"

It was there, rising straight up from the flat Martian desert towards the sky, rising up from his soul: the single red towering monolith that he knew, that he'd known, that his grandfather Ramijirring had whispered tales about to him in the flickering firelight of evening . . .

"Oolooru!"

It was the same, it was the exact same hulking silhouette: every crevice and peak was the same, the same shape that he'd known back on Earth. Exactly the same in every possible way except that it was a hundred million miles from where it ought to be . . .

How?

OOdaOOdaOOROOdada . . .

Too late to go back. Too late to do anything except heed the summons of the Dreamtime. He felt a suffocating sensation, tore the whitefella clothing from his body and let his brown skin breathe free. He gripped his spear in one hand and his knife in the other and stood tall and erect. He, Kundekundeka, son of the tribe Woombalooru, had returned to Oolooru at last!

OOdaOOdaOOROOdada . . .

153

He tore the respirator from his face and breathed pure outback air, filled his lungs with its warm salty tang. Then he flung aside his spear, stuck his knife between powerful jaws and raced towards the sandstone monolith. A mighty leap, brown fingers scrabbling for a grip, and then he was up.

OOdaOOdaOOdadadaOOROOdadaOOROOdaah . . . !

He climbed. In the gravity of Mars he practically flew up the hard rock face, bare feet and fingers soaring effortlessly up the sandstone wall. At last, high on the northern face of the huge sandstone, he came to a broad grooved hollow slope that was rippled and wrinkled like the surface of a gigantic brain, and here he rested for a time although he needed no rest. Inside his own brain, the call of the didjeridoo was louder now *OOdaOOda . . .*

Off in the distance a whine, a thrum of gathering power. Kundekundeka looked and saw some strange sort of flying machine coming towards him, some manner of . . . No! He recognized the Fleet insignia on its hull: the rocket sled from the terraform ship! They'd found out he was missing, and now they were coming after him! He reached for his knife and gripped it hard.

OOdaOOdaOOROOdada . . .

The sound jarred him back to his senses. What the hell was he doing here? What was he doing on some Martian mountain, freezing his butt without a jump-suit, trying to breathe this alien pink Martian air without a respirator? He should have suffocated by now, or frozen to . . .

OOROOdadaOOROOdaah . . . !

And if that was a didjeridoo he heard, its sound emanating from the peak of this rock that looked just like Oolooru . . . if that was a didjeridoo, then who was *playing* it?

OOda! OOda! OOdadada!

Kundekundeka broke into a run, scrambling on up the slope towards the crest, using the vegetation for cover to elude his pursuers. A kurrajong tree here, next a clump of spinifex grass . . . *grass on Mars? No such thing!* in his rush to reach the Valley of Oolooru that he instinctively knew was here, that *had* to be here. Helter-skelter he ran, not straight on, but dingo-crafty, with the sweat pouring out of his flesh, and the blood vessels pounding in his eardrums . . .

OOdaOOdaOOdadadaOOROOdadaOOROOdaah . . . !

A shadow dropped out of the Martian sky, hovering above him like some carrion-eating rocket sled, and Kundekundeka looked up in confusion and saw the helicopter no that's back on Earth I mean flying machine. He screeched in dismay and defiance, ducked beneath an overhang where the rocket sled's infra-red sensors could not see him, and he raced towards the crest of Oolooru while the chant of the didjeridoo went mad inside his brain . . .

OOdaOOdaOOROOdada . . .

OOdaOOdaOOROOdada . . .

"Oolooru!" gasped Kundekundeka as he ran. The flying machine swooped down upon him like Kuniya the she-python, its streamlined hull gleaming in the crimson aurora of its jets. Kundekundeka turned, dodged, ran faster, and then in the first fading glow of Martian sunrise he scrambled to the top of the crest, three kilometres above the surface of the planet, and looked down to see what lay beyond.

OOROOdadaOOROOdada . . .

The ground collapsed beneath him, and Kundekundeka fell, hurtling down in a shower of sandstone. Something struck his head and he lay moaning, trying to fathom where he could possibly be.

Child of the Woombalooru, child of the coolibah desert . . .

Someone else's chant was singing inside Kundekundeka's head. Confused, he staggered to his feet and found himself thinking all at once in Woombalooru and in English and some unknown tongue all together. *Wilychta*: a shelter. He was standing in a cavern shaped like the pouch of a she-wallaby. *Tiwa tjura*: distant light, strange light coming from everywhere at once and from nowhere in particular. A *fading* light, a light about to die. Kundekundeka sniffed warily: the air in this cavern was like Earth air, but mustier, and the cavern was warm. The gravity was wrong too: not Martian at all; if anything, a little heavier than Earth's gravity . . .

Child of the Woombalooru, hear me . . .

Through haggard eyes, Kundekundeka found the source of the light: an altar, a platform in the centre of the chamber. A withered figure lying on the hard stone surface, wizened fingers outstretched and sightless eyes gazing longingly towards the stars. A face that spoke, yet had no mouth. Instinctively, in his own tribal dialect, the Woombalooru tribesman introduced himself: *"Ngayulu ini Kundekundekanya."*

Yes; I know your name, for I can taste your soul. Kundekundeka, son of the tribe Woombalooru, hear my words . . .

The brown man staggered towards the figure on the slab. Body like a man, yet not a man; feet and fingers incredibly old with the life fading out of them. Face like a . . . Kundekundeka knew that face. He'd looked upon it a hundred times in the cavern paintings of his homeland, glimpsed it fleetingly on the rock walls of mighty Oolooru Stone-from-Sky. His grandfather Ramijirring had sung the ancient tales to him, of how the *Wandjina* came from the stars and went back to them, in the days beyond the Dreamtime. And now somehow Kundekundeka knew, knew without asking, that this was the very last of the ancient Wandjina who lay here before him.

Hear my words, Kundekundeka, for my time now is short . . .

Silently, the brown man huddled in the half-light at the foot of the slab.

We were many once and mighty, my people Wandjina. On a thousand thousand worlds we made our homes, observing life, watching a thousand races flourish. And one such race was your own, my child: the Woombalooru.

"Was it you who summoned me to this place?" Kundekundeka whispered. "Was it you who spoke in my dream?"

Yes. I detected Woombalooru life-strength when first you came to this planet. The means by which I sang the dream into your soul, the method by which I enabled you to survive without oxygen on the high Martian plain, the means by which I control the climate in this chamber and made this mountain assume the likeness of blessed Oolooru in your sight . . . these are all quite simple things for a race such as mine, although they required an exertion of so much of my dwindling life-strength that I fear I can remain but little longer . . .

"You brought me here . . . why?"

For selfish reasons: I am dying, and would look upon Earthchild life one last time. The words in Kundekundeka's mind were growing fainter every moment. *And now the time approaches when I must depart . . .*

"Wait!" pleaded Kundekundeka. "You have touched the stars! Your mind must contain great wisdom and knowledge. My people, the people of Earth, are just taking our first steps into space. And we have famines and disease and war and hatred and madness. Can't you please, please tell me how my people can stop these . . ."

Fool! cried the withered voice within his mind, fairly weeping with rage. *Man, man, foolish little mortal man. Do you think me a god, who can solve your race's troubles with a single cosmic Answer?*

Kundekundeka shivered in coldness and fear. "But there *must* be an Answer: a way to end death and poverty and ignorance and . . ."

Man, man, Earthchild, shall I tell you why my people Wandjina have travelled to a thousand thousand worlds? We were searching for that same Answer! For a million aeons it has eluded us. Perhaps if, instead of looking outward, to the heavens, we had looked inward. Sought the truth within ourselves . . .

Kundekundeka was silent.

But this much have I learned, said the whisper in his mind. *You must never fail to heed the summons of the Dreamtime. For of all the creatures of Earth, only the man-child and the woman-child can truly dream. And it is only the dreamers who can reach out to touch the stars . . .*

The voice in Kundekundeka's mind fell silent. And then a distant whisper spoke to him in Woombalooru: *Palunya, wiyari ngulta. Now I am done.*

Suddenly: harsh wind, a blast of cold Martian air against his face. Kundekundeka looked up in fear and found himself naked, with the air getting colder and more alien every moment.

"*Johnny!* You in there? Where in . . . *Damn!* Get that blanket here, will you?" In the thickening haze, Johnny Kundekundeka Longfellow made out the features of MacDonald, squinting at him from behind a respirator. A warm electric blanket was thrown over Kundekundeka, and without a moment's hesitation MacDonald tore the respirator from his own face and pressed it over Kundekundeka's mouth and nose.

Arnstein arrived, mad as hell. "Longfellow, you idiot! I'm going to see you court-martialled for this if it takes from now till . . ."

"With all due respect, commander, shut your trap," MacDonald growled. "Don't you see where we are? A stone chamber, carved out of the rock. Some kind of altar over there. It's an archaeological find: *life on Mars*, and Johnny here found it! He'll be a hero when we get back to Earth, and . . ."

Kundekundeka heard no more. Through half-closed eyes he saw a mound of dust on the cold stone slab: a bit of dust that had once been something very like a man and now was whirling away in the shrill Martian wind. And completely exhausted now, Kundekundeka left the waking-world and journeyed across reality's edge to the Dreamtime. For it was in the Dreamtime that he would dance among the stars . . .

This is the INDEX.

◀━━━━ . . . and THIS is the index FINGER.

An Actor Prepares	81
Aqua Viva	67
Armageddon Out of Here	78
Ballad of Ewan Owain ap Bwbytt, The	72
Bandersnatch, The	32
Beast in the Loch, The	58
Bigfoot, The	44
Blob, The	34
Bug-Eyed Monster, The	46
Bump in the Night, The	20
Centaur, The	12
Chinese Dragons, The	16
Clone, The	26
Coming Soon to a Planet Near You	71
'Dear Doctor Asimov...' (letter in rhymed verse)	75
Doin' the Prime Directive	60
Donovan's Mikado; or, I've Got a Little Lust	62
Doppelgänger, The	19
Elf, The	48
Empath, The	50
Faun, The	13
Genie in the Lamp, The	52
George Scithers (acrostic sonnet)	73
Ghoul, The	51
Gremlin and the Glitch, The	30
Happy Birthday, John Brunner	72
Heisenberg, The	18
Hollow-Earthers, The	24
I Saw You	68
Immortality	68
Invisible Man, The	38
Kraken, The	22
Little Green Men, The	40
Long-Lost First Draft of 'The Raven', The	64
Man Who Split in Twain, The	114
Marooned Off Pallas	90
Martian, The	10
Martian Walkabout	140
Missing Link, The	42
Nightmare, The	29
Ogre, The	56
'OOPS!'	76
Other, The	33
Pookah, The	36
Ruddy	69
Science Fiction (acrostic sonnet)	74
Styx and Stones	77
That Settles That	71
Thing in the Jar, The	00
Time-Traveller, The	47
Troll, The	14
Unicorn, The	41
Vampire, The	28
Vanishing Man, The	54
Yeti, The	9

www.ingramcontent.com/pod-product-compliance
Lightning Source LLC
Chambersburg PA
CBHW050752250626
47155CB00005B/2027